7

CH01466866

*Bill Tom
11th June 2014*

Tales From Portlaw
Volume Eleven: 'Two Sisters'

By
William Forde

© Copyright May 2016
By
William Forde

All text, characters, reproduction, manufacturing,
exploitation and artwork copyright
Reserved by
William Forde.

Tales From Portlaw

Volume Eleven: 'Two Sisters'

By
William Forde

Published by William Forde
May 2016

Copyright © 2016 by William Forde

All rights reserved. This book or any portion thereof may not be reproduced or used in any manner whatsoever without the express written permission of the publisher except for the use of brief quotations in a book review or scholarly journal.

ISBN-13: 978-1533061782

ISBN-10: 1533061785

Published by William Forde

www.fordefables.co.uk

Contents

Author's Foreword

I grew up on my mother's stories. Although an Irish woman of small stature and imaginative mind, stories didn't come any 'taller' than those tales told by my mother. They would stretch the bounds of one's credulity beyond the realms of possibility, and yet, she always made me 'want to believe them'.

I was born in Portlaw and when my time comes to lie at the other side of the green sod, it is my wish that one third my ashes shall be placed upon my grandparents' grave, William and Mary Fanning, along with my uncles, Willie Fanning and Johnnie Fanning who are also buried there. One third will be placed on my parent's grave, Paddy and Maureen Forde and the remainder of my ashes placed at a spot on the Haworth Moor, which holds significance for me and my wife Sheila.

Although small in size and population, Portlaw is famous for having been a 'model village' long before similar village concepts like Saltaire in West Yorkshire or Rowntrees in York were established. Although its fortune as a village of importance has waned over the years, and particularly since the closure of its last major business, the Tannery, it nevertheless remains a potent force in the minds of all of us who were born there.

I'd had dozens of books published between 1990 and 2005, at which time I had initially decided to hang up my pen. My wife Sheila however persuaded me to resume my writing of stories. I had always wanted to write short stories, so after having been persuaded to return to writing, I decided to recount some of the stories told to me by my mother long ago. Being a person with my own imagination, I have taken the germ of her tales and elaborated them with the aid of 70 years of wisdom and a splash of literary licence to come up with the final result.

Nellie and Nora Fanning are the 'Two Sisters'. In fact, they are the two most important sisters ever to come out of Portlaw. Their entrance into the world was as momentous as their influence upon it and as mysterious as their departure from it. They were two sisters with one mind, who in their later years dedicated their existence to preserve the life of Portlaw.

Enjoy.

William Forde

May 2016

Chapter One: 'The Birth of Portlaw.'

For centuries, the small village of Portlaw in County Waterford, Ireland remained a largely unpopulated place of insignificance, where it was said that more animals grazed there than man, woman or child.

One day, many centuries ago, a freak weather storm opened the heavens and over a period of forty days and forty nights, thunder and lightning bolts filled the skies. Heavy rain poured down non-stop on the green pasture below, flooding the fields and suffocating the stream that flowed beneath the stone bridge.

Though the rain that poured was concentrated within an area of one square mile, the storm that carried it could be heard sixty miles away. It was even rumoured by the people of County Mayo, that the underground seepage of flood water from Portlaw had created disturbance on the holy mount of Crough Patrick, waking the nest of snakes that Saint Patrick is said to have cast into a deep sleep way back in the fifth century, before burying them beneath the mountain base.

As the downpour swelled, the surging waters continued to widen the banks of the stream, transforming it to the status and size of waterway that afterwards became known as the River Clodiagh. Within two weeks of constant downpour, the River Clodiagh united its waters with the neighbouring River Suir that ran parallel. The two became ever-closer neighbours of nature, even though a distance of three miles had previously kept them separated for centuries.

This widening of the Clodiagh encouraged a dozen travelling families of gypsy origin to settle in the place named Port Cladach, a village that was later to be known throughout Ireland as Portlaw.

The families took up occupation in the surrounding pasture and green belt land. Having no trade to call upon apart from the few skills they had learned on the open road, they hoped to earn a modest living raising a few cows, chickens and sheep, and making wooden pegs to sell from door to door. If such trade proved insufficient to feed them, they planned to sharpen the tools of passers-by on their whetstone and read the palms of the most superstitious to supplement their income.

~~~

Over the next two hundred years, this small village gradually grew in population until it became a thriving community. It eventually came into prominence after the Malcomson family built a cotton mill at its centre that employed all of the town's workers.

The Malcomsons were a Quaker family and their religious ideals affected most of the townsfolk of Portlaw. They also built industrial houses and social networks as part of the planned town that still forms a central part of the streetscape today.

By the 1840's, 'The Portlaw Cotton Factory' was spinning, weaving, bleaching, dying and printing. The hours were long and though the wages at the time were better than could be earned in most parts of Ireland, the potato famine that was soon to blight the entire country, fast approached.

The American Civil War in 1861 was a bad blow to the Portlaw factory. Raw cotton surpluses dwindled and after the war, the New America imposed tariffs on Irish cotton. This signalled the end of the Malcolmson business empire. The cotton factory was taken over by 'The Portlaw Spinning Company.' That factory also closed and eventually in 1932, 'The Irish Tanners Ltd' secured the site and in September 1935, 'The Portlaw Tannery' officially opened.

Despite having been placed on the map by the Malcomson family and their cotton mill many years earlier, Portlaw was not to become world famous until the two sisters, Nellie and Nora Fanning blessed the parish with their presence. Indeed, many came to believe that the Fanning sisters were largely responsible for placing Portlaw on the international map and giving it a worldwide reputation that would live a thousand years!

Chapter Two: 'The Birth of the Fanning Sisters: April 1916.'

Nellie and Nora Fanning were born at the Maternity Hospital in County Waterford on Easter Monday, April 24th, 1916. As they awoke to new life outside their mother's womb, 'The Easter Rising' was taking place 120 miles away in Dublin City and the dead bodies of their co-twins lay wrapped in a hospital shroud nearby.

Earlier that morning at 11am, about 1,250 members of Irish Volunteers and Irish Citizen Army started to assemble across Dublin City. Over the next hour, they began to occupy strategic buildings in the city. By noon, the Volunteers had seized weapons from the Magazine Fort in Dublin's Phoenix Park and twenty minutes later, they marched into the General Post Office and established the building as the headquarters of the Rising, after flying the rebel flag of the Tricolour from its rooftop.

At 12.45, a proclamation, declaring Ireland a Republic on behalf of the 'Provisional Government was read out. Not all Dubliners celebrated the uprising. Great Britain was at war with Germany at the time and thousands of Irish families had relatives fighting for the British in Europe.

The uprising in Dublin was to last a full seven days. On Saturday, April 29th, 1916, the rebels surrendered in the early afternoon. The Rising was over and the

British arrested a total of 3,430 men and 79 women. The dead and wounded tally exceeded 1,350.

Back in the Waterford Maternity Hospital, a further two deaths had taken place, along with two births of surviving twins.

~~~

Thirty-two weeks earlier, Mary Fanning learned that she was pregnant and was expecting quads. While initially overjoyed to be the prospective mother of four instead of the more usual one, Mary soon came face to face with the cold cruelty of life and death.

Eight weeks into her pregnancy, upon examination, the doctor told Mary that two of the foetuses were failing to thrive in the womb and were most unlikely to survive the full gestation period. The medics said that if the two least nourished foetuses did survive until the moment of their birth, which was most unlikely, all four of the quads would probably suffer in consequence.

Poor Mary, having recently separated from her husband faced most of her pregnancy alone, apart from the help of her stepmother, Nancy. She felt twisted and torn in a torrent of trepidation, hoping for the best, but fearing the worst.

Knowing that if the two feeblest of her foetuses lived, then the lives of all four would be at risk, left Mary's motherly instincts unable to pray for either outcome. She eventually resigned herself to placing her fate and that of her unborn children in the hands of the Lord.

As feared, Mary left the Maternity Hospital with only two of the original four foetuses she had carried inside her for thirty-two weeks. The surviving two baby girls were low in weight, but otherwise healthy in all other ways. Both mother and babies stayed in hospital for an extra week.

Upon return to her home in Portlaw, Mary carried two babies in her arms and kept the other two sisters who had died in her heart. She could not reconcile her bitter and ironic combination of grief and celebration, being fully aware that within the week, she would be attending the funeral of her two unborn children.

Chapter Three: 'Mary Lannon Craves Motherhood'

Nellie and Nora Fanning's mother had been born Mary Lannon in Clonmel, County Tipperary on December 8th, 1892. She was the eldest of thirteen children, ten of whom survived beyond their infancy. She was born on one of the Marian Feast Days of the Roman Catholic Church, 'The Immaculate Conception of the Blessed Virgin Mary,' and was therefore, naturally named after the Blessed Virgin. Her mother was Maureen and her father Harry worked as the second hand to a local Smithy.

Ever since her early childhood years, Mary Lannon had but one dream, to become a mother. She knew that from all the roles in the world, the one she most craved was that of 'motherhood'. She always felt like a mother, thought like a mother and even learned to perform those household roles that mothers are born to do.

Mary had always tried to live up to the worthiness of her baptismal name. She revered the Blessed Virgin even as much as she revered Jesus himself, and had it not been for her obsession with motherhood, her natural devoutness would have no doubt led to her joining the sisterhood in her teens and eventually becoming a nun.

Indeed, virtually all of Mary's childhood witnessed her enacting the role of motherhood. She helped her mum at every opportunity, looking after her younger siblings and essentially becoming 'second mother' in the household by the age of nine years. Whenever she played her games, it was always a game played with her younger siblings or other children.

No sooner than she had entered teenage years, Mary's mind was filled with one thought only, that of motherhood. Instead of dreaming of boys or being attentive to her lessons in class, Mary would spend most of her days looking out the window and daydreaming of the future when she would have children of her own to tend to and educate.

The nuns who taught the pupils were constantly reprimanding Mary for her persistent daydreaming. They were extremely strict in the imposition of discipline and were quick to use the swish of the cane in the event of inattentiveness or any talking back.

It did not seem to matter whether it be boy or girl being punished, all pupils were caned in public view of the rest of the class. Whether boy or girl, each received the swish across their bottom; and as if to add further shame to the punishment, the girls would have their dresses raised over their heads before they received their caning.

Whenever a girl received her public punishment, the boys would gawp as they strained their eyeballs seeking closer sight of her knickers or anything beneath. Many pupils believed that by allowing boys to witness the caning of girls in such a public manner, the nuns got a second whack at punishment duties.

Prior to caning any girl, the teaching nuns would always instruct the boys in class to look away, but few ever did. It was as though their need for biological advancement and the exercising of their male curiosity level led them to ignore the instructions of their teachers and suppress their fear of reprisal.

Before she had reached her fourteenth year of life, Mary planned upon getting married as soon as possible after leaving school. Above all else, she wanted investiture of the status of motherhood, and if the prerequisite for such a position in society were one of marriage, then she would happily suffer the consequences by wearing the wedding veil and taking wifely vows. It mattered not whom she married or who the father of her children would be, so long as he was a good Catholic man who was neither a drunkard, wife beater nor child abuser; and preferably a man who would not make too many sexual demands of her.

~~~

All of Mary's courtship relationships quickly failed because of her innocence in the ways of the world. She was particularly unfortunate being the subject to the teenage law of 'double jeopardy.' You see, Mary believed that one could be a good girl and still have a good time in the process; a view that every one of her boyfriends strongly disagreed with!

Naturally, after a goodly time of familiarity had passed between Mary and her current boyfriend, while she seemed happy to maintain the 'status quo', the boyfriend simply wanted to move on and progress their relationship to the next stage. As far as Mary was concerned however, all seemed to be going swimmingly, whereas all her boyfriends would beg to differ!

During any courtship period with Mary, not one of her frustrated boyfriends ever managed to get beyond first base with her. You see, Mary had her boundaries of propriety and she stuck to them rigidly. The extent of her commitment to any boyfriend would never exceed that of the holding of hands in private and a peck on the cheek in public.

Having always led a sheltered life, Mary could not possibly know of the expectations of conventional courtship between boy and girl. Until she became a married woman, Mary continued to believe that showing any male what lay beneath her dress as being undignified and wholly improper.

In truth, Mary much preferred to be in the company of girls than boys and she certainly considered it less troublesome. In her state of worldly ignorance, when it came to the expectations of teenage boys, Mary paid absolutely no regard to the correlation between their persistence for her to reveal all and their overflowing testosterone levels.

'You may have been educated by the nuns' one of her boyfriends who left her after three months with nothing to show for it remarked, 'but there's no need to behave like a bloody nun! No need to take the vow of chastity!'

Unfortunately, for her string of boyfriends, Mary's strict moral upbringing and Catholic beliefs led to her holding out at crucial junctures of the courtship game. Mary wanted children above all else, but would never have considered having sex before marriage as a legitimate means of acquiring them. For her, touching tongues while kissing would introduce her to satanic practices of the flesh, and to risk a child being born outside the bonds of marriage would have guaranteed her a place in hell!

In fact, had Mary considered herself as blessed as her namesake was, she would have been more than willing to have an immaculate conception announced to her by the Angel Gabriel!"

~~~

During her teenage years, Mary's longing to have a child grew so unbearable that had it not been for the shame attached, she may have succumbed to having sex with her boyfriend, however unpleasant the experience might prove to be.

The only proper way out of her dilemma seemed to be getting married as soon as it was legally permissible, but she knew that to persuade her strict parents to allow her to marry so young would be nigh on impossible. After all, she was their eldest daughter and had firmly established herself in the role of a mini mother within the household; the chief protector and mentor to all her younger siblings.

Were she to up sticks and leave the parental abode, her parents would miss her daily contribution to the smooth running of their family network so much that it would naturally lead them to prevent her. To them, though mini mother she undoubtedly was, she was still their little girl whom no man was worthy of.

Chapter Four: 'Mary Lannon meets Paddy Fanning: June, 1909.'

The first time Mary Lannon met Paddy Fanning from Kilkenny was at the Waterford Fair in the summer of 1909 when she was sixteen going on seventeen. Two thoughts preoccupied her at the time, marriage and motherhood.

Mary had earlier that day been given the task of looking after three of her younger siblings for the afternoon while their mother visited a poorly brother in the Waterford hospital.

Mary had left school one and a half years earlier, but instead of seeking full time work outside the family home, she instead continued in her mini mother's role of looking after her young siblings who were yet not old enough to attend school. She also took in washing and ironing from the neighbours to earn a few extra shillings. This part-time work provided Mary with some pin money, and the fact that she was able to perform this additional work from her parent's house enabled her to keep a watchful eye on her younger siblings simultaneously.

The Waterford Fair was an annual event attended by over twenty thousand visitors. While many a famer showed their cattle at the fair, there were breeders galore of all manner of sheep and dogs and anxious owners seeking blue ribbons for their pets, along with vegetable growers wanting to take home the Silver Cup for the largest specimen in show. There was even one huge tent given over to the judging of bread cakes and homemade jams and honey made by the fair hands of Waterford women.

Part way through the afternoon, seven-year-old Patrick Lannon, who loved dogs, slipped into the tent next-door showing the different breeds of hounds when Mary was not looking. One minute she was holding Patrick in one hand and his six-year-old sister Teresa in the other, when she spotted some jars of honey being sold off. Mary knew that her mother loved honey and decided to buy her a jar as a surprise.

When Mary next looked, she quickly realised that her brother Patrick had slipped her hand. For the next ten minutes, Mary franticly searched for her young brother and started to become frightened after her search of three nearby tents proved futile.

Just as Mary started to look around for some Marshall or Garda for assistance, she spotted her brother Patrick holding the hand of a male stranger. Patrick seemed to have been crying and for a moment, Mary feared that the stranger might have tried to abduct the boy.

She quickly ran towards her brother calling out his name. "Patrick…Patrick, over here. I'm here, Patrick!" The stranger released Patrick from his grasp and allowed him to run towards his older sister. Expecting the stranger to run off, 'having been found out,' Mary was surprised to see the man approach her. He gently smiled reassuringly to see her and Patrick reunited.

When young Patrick ran into the arms of his older sister, Mary first started to embrace him and then quickly found herself scolding the boy for having left her side. "You silly boy," Mary said to Patrick in a stern voice, adding, "Don't you ever do that again! You had me worried sick. Why did you go off with that strange man, anything could have happened? You might have finished up stolen and sold on to the travellers or you could even have been killed and thrown down some abandoned well!"

When Mary had finished berating her young brother for his foolishness, the strange man approached closer and started to explain.

"I saw the boy in yonder tent. He was on the verge of tears," he told Mary. "He muttered that he'd lost Mary, which I presume to be yourself and I was simply staying with him to stop him coming to any harm until we found you again. Now that he's found you, I'll be away. I know where I'm not wanted!"

Mary felt foolish and ungrateful for her initial response to the kind stranger. "Please accept my apology if I came across hostile," she said adding, "it's just that he was entrusted to my charge for the afternoon by my mother and.....well...she'd never have forgiven me if any harm had come to him as a result of my negligence."

"It was nothing," the stranger replied after graciously receiving the fair maiden's apology. "By the way, my name is Paddy Fanning and I'm pleased to meet you."

"And I'm very pleased to make your acquaintance also, Paddy; I'm Mary Lannon from Clonmel."

As Mary spoke to Paddy, she looked him over with the eyes of a young girl in search of a good husband and father.

The stranger was around five feet and eight inches tall and was quite muscular, with strong arms, hairy chest and wide shoulders. His face was ruggedly handsome and Mary judged him to be in his early twenties. Overall, Mary thought him wholesome in every way imaginable.

"Walk with us," Mary invited the stranger. "I have to buy the children some afternoon tea and buns and the least I can do is to share the pot with you."

Paddy Fanning agreed to join them for tea and buns and before the afternoon had ended and evening approached, Mary and Patrick each believed that someone had entered their lives that day who would stay a part of it for many years to come.

~~~

As Mary and her younger siblings travelled back home to Clonmel that evening on the bus, the children looked out the window while young Teresa slept on Mary's shoulder.

Throughout the two-hour journey, Mary thought sweet thoughts about Paddy whom she had met that afternoon. Mary was a strong believer in destiny being decided by the angels in heaven and fate alighting on one when least expected. She sensed her destiny in the making. She felt an intervention in her life, bringing her and Paddy into contact with each other that afternoon. Something inside told her that Paddy was the one to father the children she badly wanted and that he would make a grand husband.

As for the twenty-two-year old Kilkenny man, when Paddy left the Waterford Show that afternoon, he also sensed he had met the girl he would one day marry. Though Mary was a mere sixteen-year-old slip of a girl, her overall looks, speech, mannerisms and the confident way she handled herself made her appear more mature in years than she actually was. Paddy had assessed her to be eighteen, going on nineteen.

Paddy had given Mary his Kilkenny address, just in case she fancied dropping him a line at some future date. Not having provided him with her parent's address in Clonmel essentially placed Mary in the driver's seat regarding the possibility of any future contact between the two of them. This made Mary feel more in control and gave her time to make up her mind, while Paddy on the other hand, knew that if he heard from Mary again, it would be of her choosing and not his!

During the next month, Paddy held many feelings of doubt and uncertainty as Mary struggled to do what was right for all concerned. While Mary considered her decision whether to make contact with Paddy again, the Kilkenny man eventually resigned himself to the belief that she had simply forgotten him. One way or another, both could not get the other out of their mind.

They had met briefly and but once, and had shared a pot of tea and hardly spoken, yet upon parting, each had left an indelible impression upon the other that this meeting would not be their last. Both Mary and Paddy felt the sensation of having touched each other's soul. It was a touch that simply would not go away after the couple had parted.

Chapter Five: 'Mary's and Paddy's Courtship'

Three months passed by before Mary decided to write to Paddy in Kilkenny. Though having been sorely tempted to write the day after their first meeting, Mary decided to think hard upon the matter for the next two weeks. She told herself that if at the end of that time she still felt the same, she would take the plunge and reinitiate contact with the Kilkenny man. However, as so often happens fate, took the decision from her hands.

One week after returning from the Waterford Show, Mary's father, Harry Lannon suffered a very bad accident when a runaway horse and cart ran through the street towards a mother walking her pram across the road.

Seeing the accident about to happen and anticipating its consequences, without a second thought for himself, Mary's father ran headlong towards the mother and pram as fast as his legs would carry him. Arriving just in time, he pushed both mother and child out of the way, mere seconds before the horse knocked him to the ground, trampled him, and the cartwheels ran over his prostrate body, crushing his chest and breaking numerous bones in the process.

During the next week, Mary's dad fought for his life in the hospital. One of the broken ribs in his chest had punctured a lung and there was severe damage done to his spine and back where the cartwheels had run over.

Her father remained in hospital for five weeks and though the feared spinal damage had not proved severe enough to prevent him ever walking again, one of his legs had been so badly damaged that he would never walk again unaided. Harry Lannon would need crutches for the rest of his life and his walk would forever mirror that of an ungainly hobble. He now also had a weakened back. This back injury caused him continuous pain and made sure that he would never work manually again.

Forever a proud man who had always worked hard to support his wife and large family, Harry Lannon worried greatly who would now provide for his wife and children, now that he could no longer work to support them. He started to mend bicycles for the other villagers, as this was lighter work he could do, and from the premises of his home shed. But however long his hours of work and however many bikes he fixed and wheel punctures he repaired, the amount of money he earned represented no more than the pin money of a married woman's part-time job.

It was eventually decided that his wife Maureen would go back out to work in the town bakery as she could earn more to bring home than her sixteen year old daughter, Mary. Her daughter Mary subsequently became the 'number one' Mama of the household during her mother's daily absence.

Poor Mary felt trapped. All her life she had craved to look after children and now that she'd been given the sole charge of nine of them between the hours of 5.30am and 4.pm when her mum was out of the family home, in her heart of hearts, she didn't want all this responsibility.

You see, though Mary had always wanted to mother children, she had always dreamed of mothering her own children. Mothering her brothers and sisters was not quite the same!

Following her father's accident, Mary became quickly aware of the necessary changes in the household that would now be required. Being the dutiful child she was, Mary knew that the greater burden of change would fall to her. She knew where her duty lay during the immediate years ahead. Her present responsibilities fate had mapped out and prime role was clear; to play the part of mother in the parental abode to her younger siblings and not within her own marital home!

The only spare time that Mary had for herself during the months ahead were a few hours on a Sunday afternoon. Her mother now worked throughout the week and Saturday morning at the bakery. The early start was very tiring on Mary's mum and when she finished work for the week on a Saturday noon, she would be exhausted and needing rest. Maureen Lannon only started to come round again by Sunday morning, yet appreciated how hard her daughter, Mary, worked in her absence.

Mary's hard work and lack of leisure time from one week to the next eventually induced sufficient guilt in her mother to suggest to her daughter that in future she have Sunday noon until 8pm free to do or go wherever she willed.

Maureen Lannon knew that other sixteen-year-old girls, with whom Mary had attended school, would be out at weekends having fun, whereas her daughter, not yet seventeen, was working her fingers to the bone all week long, looking after her siblings.

When Mary's mother gave her Sunday's off, the young woman immediately knew how she would spend her first free Sunday. That night when the household was asleep, Mary got out pen and paper and wrote a letter to Paddy Fanning that she would post first thing the following morning:

Number 17, Davis Street,

Clonmel

October 4th, 1909

Dear Paddy,

You have probably forgotten me, but I am the young woman you met at the Waterford Show in June. I am the one who lost her young brother in the crowd, and whom you kindly found.

You gave me your address in Kilkenny and asked me to write to you upon my return home. I did intend to write a week or so after the Show, but family circumstances, which I will not go into now, prevented me doing so.

If you would still like to meet me again, I would be prepared to see you in Waterford on the next Sunday afternoon you are available. I am sorry, but my home circumstances dictate that any future meetings between us must take place on a Sunday afternoon. I can be in

Waterford by 3pm on the bus from Clonmel any Sunday and will meet you by the clock.

If you do not want to meet up again, I perfectly understand. Thank you for returning my brother Patrick safely to me.'

Mary Lannon.

The next day, Mary posted off the letter. It was five days before she received a reply. Never having had a letter from Paddy previously, she was unable to know if it was he who had penned it, but seeing a Kilkenny postmark on the envelope, Mary had no reason to suppose it was from another.

Paddy had written his letter of reply in scribbled hand and its poor grammar, lack of punctuation and spelling mistakes identified his obvious lack of schooling. As Mary read the briefest of letters, her heart beat anxiously. The letter simply said:

'Dearest Mary Lannon. Why did you keep me waiting so long. Of corse I want to see you again. Wood Sunday the 17th October be ok. If I dont hear back I will meet you at the bus stop near the clock.'

Paddy Fanning.

Mary concealed the letter on her person and smiled secretly as she went about her childminding, housekeeping and domestic chores. It was Thursday, October 14th. Only three days to go before she would meet up with Paddy again. She had not felt so frightened yet so happy previously, all at the same time. She was happy to be seeing Paddy again, but apprehensive that their meeting might not go as well as she hoped it would.

~~~

Mary arrived in Waterford on the Sunday of the 17th as planned. She had put on the best clothes she possessed, which were in keeping with the weather; a yellow cardigan, gold coloured skirt, brown shoes and brown coat. Mary had left the house looking like her parents' sixteen-year-old daughter, but stepped off the bus, looking far more mature, having applied red lipstick and a bit of rouge to her cheeks along the way.

As the bus arrived in Waterford, she could see Paddy by the clock on the waterfront. The clock was a popular meeting place for all manner of folk. Children, teenagers and adults used the clock as a regular meeting place. Lovers also used it as a contact point, along with the occasional married man arranging a clandestine meeting with his woman friend.

As Mary looked at Paddy, she saw that he was holding the handlebars of a bicycle meant for two, a tandem. Mary smiled at Paddy as she approached and let him be the first to talk. Despite not being the talkative kind, wherever a fair maiden was involved, Paddy would always know what not to say. If he tried to talk too much he could easily become lost for words. Like his letters, Paddy kept his words to an absolute minimum and once Mary realised this, she kept the conversation flowing.

Paddy had borrowed the tandem from a friend and had ridden it the thirty-three miles from his home address in Kilkenny to Waterford.

"I thought we'd ride out to Tramore," he said.

"That sounds marvellous, it's been a good few years since I've been out that way," Mary replied.

One hour later, the couple were in Tramore. It was only after Paddy had asked Mary if she would like a drink at the corner pub that her look of surprise indicated to him that she might not be as old as she looked.

"You're not old enough to drink in the pub are you, Mary Lannon?" he asked.

"I'm only seventeen years old...well...I'm almost seventeen and will be so on December 8th," Mary said sheepishly.

Paddy looked at his female companion and smiled. Boys had often smiled at Mary, but never quite in the same way that Paddy smiled at her now! It the kind of smile only a mysterious man might make; the kind of smile that expected everything, yet one that asked for nothing! Despite Mary's lack of serious courtship experience, Paddy did not need to identify the thoughts inside his head when he next looked at her. His look required no words to know their meaning and told her plainly all that she needed to know. That inner knowledge excited, yet made her feel distinctly uncomfortable.

Sensing her innocent awkwardness, Paddy acted the perfect gentleman that day and was courteous in the extreme. The day was a perfect success all round and it was only when Patrick put Mary back on the early evening bus for Clonmel and gently kissed her on the lips, with one hand respectfully on her waist, that the first intimate contact was made between the couple.

Mary and Patrick had arranged to meet at the same spot two Sundays hence. They agreed that if the other had not arrived one hour after the appointed time, each was to assume that something unavoidable had cropped up and that they could not come as planned. In such an event, they agreed to meet up two Sundays after, at the same time and place.

Two weeks later as planned, the couple met up again by the clock in Waterford near Mary's bus stop. Paddy had brought the tandem again and the couple went out to Tramore once more. Only this time they did not cycle the road that took them to the beach, but instead took the high road towards the 'Metal Man'.

Though he was not as educated as much as Mary was, Paddy did know his local history. Besides, Mary had no inkling of the significance that the 'Metal Man' had already played in Paddy's life.

Paddy's mother had told her son one night after she had drunk too much stout, that whereas all children knew where they had been born and on which day, month and year, very few knew precisely where they had been conceived. His mother had told Paddy that he had been a much-wanted bairn and had been 'brought about' within sight of the 'Metal Man' in Tramore. While Paddy was ignorant as to the meaning of 'conception' or being 'brought about' at the first time of hearing these terms, he never forgot his mother's words.

Paddy told Mary that the most prominent feature of Tramore Bay was the 'Metal Man.' He pointed out that the construction was a large figure made out of cast metal and pointed seawards from one of three pillars. Lloyds of London, the firm who insured ships worldwide, had erected it in 1823. Its purpose was to warn seafarers away from dangerous shallow waters after a number of shipwrecks had occurred. Two more pillars sit on the headland opposite, Brownstown Head.

There are many myths and legends surrounding the 'Metal Man', but the one that appealed to most Irish ears, especially Mary's, was the hopping story, which Paddy related to her. Paddy said, "If a woman hopped barefoot around the base of the 'Metal Man' three times, she would be married within the year."

The 'Metal Man' became a favourite spot where Mary and Paddy visited most Sundays they met. It was extremely quiet and apart from the occasional courting couple that came by, Mary and Paddy would spend most Sunday picnics there without seeing another soul.

~~~

It was during one sunny Sunday afternoon in May when Mary and Paddy next found themselves picnicking in a field by the 'Metal Man'. The farmer who owned it had left the field fallow. The grass had grown high and provided an ideal location for many a courting couple to kiss and cuddle away from the view of onlookers and rabbit hunters.

Mary and Paddy had made a nice comfortable clearing to picnic, after which they just idled the afternoon hours away, laid beside each other sunbathing. While Paddy was far from the best of speakers or writers, when it came to courting, he was the most adventurous of explorers.

During the months since the couple had first met, the degree of intimacy that Mary had been prepared to go along with was farther than she'd ever gone before, and as far as she believed, farther than any unmarried Catholic girl should ever be prepared to go. Paddy had taught her to kiss and during their most amorous moments, he would baptise her in tongues.

In fact, Mary got so accustomed to their French kissing that she began to like it much more than she would ever let on, even to herself.

Although a patient man in the courtship stakes, Paddy soon recognised the reservations of Mary to engage in some practices of the courtship process before her time, so he became prepared to play the long game. He had decided to bide his time in the belief that Mary would eventually prove to be a willing lover. If he did not rush his colleen, Paddy reckoned that in time, Mary would reward his patience by being prepared to give all for the sake of love and continued companionship.

Mary had often allowed Paddy to stroke her breasts though never feel them bare, only over her blouse top. Try as she may to deny the occasional stirrings that Paddy was capable of arousing in her more easily and more often now, Mary could not shut out a hidden yearning deep inside. The pleasure came from changes in her own body and not the body of Paddy. She was like a dormant volcano that was making ready to erupt into full-blown womanhood.

Now, when Paddy ran his hand across her blouse slowly and tantalisingly, the hardening of her nipples beneath could not deny the pleasurable feeling she had for so long repressed, but could no longer hold back. She even discovered that she could produce the same sensations when she stroked her own breasts and lower body parts.

Each time Paddy placed his hand beneath her dress, found her knee and slowly moved his hand up it, while part of her wanted him to carry on to see how it would feel at journey's end, Mary took fright and prevented its arrival. The automatic removal of his hand by her indicated that she was not yet ready to abandon all resistance to the maintenance of her maidenhood.

When it did eventually happen, it was on a day when it was least expected.

~~~

Mary missed her next Sunday meeting with Paddy and he received no letter from her saying why. As the couple had previously agreed, he turned up two Sundays later at the appointed hour by the clock on the waterfront.

Paddy waited for the bus to empty and was bitterly disappointed not to see Mary on it. Just as he was about to leave, one of the passengers from Clonmel approached Paddy and after ascertaining his identity, gave him a brief note from Mary. Paddy thanked her and eagerly read the note. It was short and to the point and said:

'Dear Paddy,

I am so sorry, but cannot come today. My mother died a few weeks ago and as you can imagine, there has been a lot to see to, with the burial and everything else. I will try to get into Waterford in two weeks' time if I can, but please understand if I am not there.'

Love Mary x

~~~

Two weeks later, Paddy went to meet the Clonmel bus in Waterford and was overjoyed to see Mary get off it. Mary ran to embrace Paddy with tears in her eyes as soon as she saw him waiting there for her.

"There…there lass,' a concerned Paddy said softly. 'I'm here now, lass."

Paddy gave Mary a brief kiss on the cheek and they went into a nearby café on the waterfront to have a pot of tea and a long talk.

Mary said. "Ma passed away suddenly two days after we last met." At the mention of her mother's name, Mary started to cry again, this time more openly than before. She did not attempt to conceal her distress other than by the judicious placing of a handkerchief to her mouth whenever she was in danger of sobbing loud.

Mary told Paddy that two days after they had last met; her mother had collapsed at her place of work. Initially, the man who owned the bakery thought she had probably fainted with the heat, but after numerous attempts to bring her back round, it became apparent that she had mysteriously died on the job.

Given the suddenness of her death and the unexplained nature of it, an autopsy was subsequently carried out. It found that Maureen Lannon had suffered a massive brain haemorrhage. Her husband

Harry was informed that an artery in the brain had burst and she simply bled out, killing the surrounding brain cells that controlled her breathing and the functioning of the heart; leading to a severe stroke. The only consolation was that death was certainly instantaneous.

After her mother's death, Mary, being the eldest female in the large family, now had a greater responsibility to mother the surviving members of it.

"What a responsibility to put on a young woman's shoulders!" Paddy thought as Mary spoke about recent events.

The couple stayed in Waterford City that afternoon instead of cycling out to Tramore. Mary was both glad of Paddy's company and his reassuring arm around her waist as they walked and talked across the bridge before walking back again and having another trip to the teahouse.

When Paddy put her back on the bus that evening, it was with a heavy heart. Neither knew when Mary could get out to Waterford again. Paddy said he'd still come into Waterford every second Sunday, even if it took six months before Mary could come back there again for their Sunday afternoon meetings.

As Mary travelled home that evening, she cried salty tears, part joy and part sorrowful. She felt happy for having met such an understanding man in Paddy from Kilkenny. She considered herself lucky to have landed herself a patient man, given the uncertainty of her circumstances and any normal future they might have together. The bitter tears of sorrow were for the death of her beloved mother and the invalid state of her dear father.

Chapter Six: 'First Blood'

Over the following five months, Mary was able to meet up with Paddy a mere three times. Without her mother no longer being there to help with the children and household tasks, Mary seemed never to stop. She was working fifteen hours a day, seven days a week!

Her father was no longer able to give her a hand due to his disability and physical handicap, but he could see the toll that such a heavy responsibility was having on his eldest daughter.

~~~

Since his wife had died, Harry Lannon had gradually grown closer in his affections to a woman called Nancy Perkings, who was his second cousin. Nancy was four years older than Harry was, but looked ten years younger than her actual age, largely because she had never given birth or had experienced the burden of rearing children. The one thing that enjoined Harry and Nancy more than any other was their mutual love of family, plus the fact that each had lost their spouse to an early death.

Nancy had been a widow for the past six years. Her husband had died as the result of an industrial accident. While both Nancy and her husband would have liked to have children, Shamus Perkings was never able to produce fertile sperm. Nancy therefore suppressed her maternal feelings for most of her married life and it was only after the death of her husband when she found an outlet for them.

As a young woman, Nancy had planned to become an infant teacher, but part way through her teaching course, she dropped out and married Shamus Perkings.

It was never known for sure why Nancy had left her teaching course before getting married, but it was thought by those in the know that Shamus had put the pressure on her for them to marry as soon as possible, as he'd no intention of waiting three years for Nancy to finish a teachers' course of learning and instruction.

Whereas Shamus was in most ways reported to be a good man, a patient man he most certainly wasn't! After his death, Nancy had the opportunity to help at the local infant school whenever one of the teachers was ill. She enjoyed being surrounded by children and let it be known to the Head that she would willingly stand in as a helper whenever they needed her services. To tell the truth, Nancy enjoyed the school experience and caring for children so much that she would willingly have worked there free.

~~~

After the death of Mary's mother, Nancy had been the first neighbour to offer her services during those early days when all the Lannon family were grieving heavily. Nancy attended the same Catholic Church as the Lannon family and would walk back down the hill with Harry, Mary and the other nine children after Sunday mass.

Within a short space of time, Nancy had become a regular visitor to the Lannon household. She would invariably turn up with a pie she had baked or some item of clothing she had spotted in the market place that would fit one of the children. Nancy seemed to love her contact with all the children of the household and was delighted in the manner they all took to her.

With such a large family of siblings to fend for, Mary was glad to allow Nancy to do the odd task minding some of her brothers or sisters while she did some other household chore.

Without realising what was happening, Nancy's services of good will were becoming a regular and indispensable part of the Lannon household and over a brief period, her presence and her contributions gradually became more accepted by all unthinkingly.

Being too busy to notice all household activity, Mary failed to spot the ever-closer union that was developing between her father and Nancy. Though she did not see it, when nobody else was looking, Harry and Nancy would hold hands for a brief moment or look at each other in that way that only married couples are supposed to glance when they share adult thoughts and secrets from other family members.

It was only a matter of time when Mary's father said to her one Sunday noon after attending Mass, "You never go out for the afternoon anymore on a Sunday, Mary."

Mary looked at him and replied, "How can I go out when there's nine children to care for and all the meals to make and clothes to wash and darn?" Mary asked.

"I'm sure that Nancy will look after us all a few hours, Mary, if you want a Sunday afternoon off, won't you Nancy?" her father said as he looked at Nancy nearby.

"Of course I will," Nancy, who was near enough to overhear, remarked. "You get yourself off, Mary. You deserve a break. Ever since your dear mother passed away suddenly, you have been stuck in this house all week long, month in and month out. It must be unhealthy for a young woman of your age to be in the house every minute of the day. Have you no friends you'd like to see or places you want to go?"

Mary could hardly believe her ears. There was simply no way she intended to pass up this golden opportunity by turning down the offer made by her father and Nancy to start having Sunday afternoons off again. Without speaking a word, her eyes started to well up with tears and she threw her arms around Nancy.

"That's settled then," her father said smilingly. "Starting next Sunday, you will have the day to yourself again after Mass."

Mary was over the moon. She quickly went to her room and wrote a letter to Paddy saying she would meet him next Sunday in the usual place and nothing would prevent her being there. She posted the letter that evening before retiring for the day and went to bed the happiest young woman in Clonmel.

~~~

The following Sunday, Mary arrived in Waterford off the bus with a heart so light that upon seeing Paddy, the smile that instantly broke out across her face could not disguise how happy she was to be there. Without a second thought of being in full public view,

Mary flung her arms around Paddy's neck and kissed him more fulsomely than they had ever kissed previously in public view.

As they mounted the tandem and headed off towards Tramore, the couple smiled incessantly and looked forward to the day ahead.

It was a warm day and they had much to talk about, not having seen each other for a good many weeks now. Mary had bought a new dress to look her best and the wider flare in the cut of it, which was all the fashion, showed off her shapely legs to best effect.

When the couple arrived at the 'Metal Man', they made their way to their favourite spot in the farmer's field and after laying down a chequered blanket, Paddy kissed Mary.

Both embraced passionately and before Mary knew it, she found herself with her new dress riding high above her thighs and her knickers lowered. Paddy was eager to make love. Though the moment was riper than it had ever been for making love, Paddy did not intend to take Mary without her full awareness and apparent willingness. Paddy looked at his colleen beneath him and eagerly awaited her response to his silent wish.

"Oh yes, Paddy. Yes! Do it now, Paddy, do it now!" Mary whispered sweetly.

Mary wanted to taste the full experience of making love with a man. Paddy entered Mary and they gently started to make love. Knowing Mary to be a virgin, Paddy deliberately exercised consideration as he became more aroused. Mary was so pleased that this was so and while she found the overall experience pleasant at its height of arousal, she nevertheless found it painful enough to be pleased when it was over!

Chapter Seven: 'Wedding Bells on the Horizon'

Over the next three months, Mary and Paddy met most Sundays in Waterford. The couple found it more difficult to keep the frequency of their meetings fortnightly, when all each did when they were apart and in their own homes was to think about the other.

When Mary's eighteenth birthday came around on Thursday, December 8th, 1910, she was happier than her father had ever known her to be. About three weeks earlier, Nancy had asked Mary outright if she had a young man whom she saw. Her father was in earshot at the time when Mary replied.

"I've been seeing a Kilkenny man called Paddy Fanning for the best part of the past year now, whenever I can," Mary replied coyly, adding, "On a Sunday afternoon. We meet up in Waterford and usually go walking or on a cycle ride."

"I'm pleased for you, Mary," Nancy replied. "Me and your dad wondered how you spent most Sunday afternoons and seeing the smile on your face when you walked back in the door on your return, we half guessed it was a young man who was responsible for putting the gladness there."

"I wouldn't particularly call Paddy a young man; I'd say he was more 'a man's man,' much more than a young man," Mary replied, adding, "He's twenty-three!"

"What does he do for a living? What's his job?" Mary's father asked.

"He's just a labourer like everyone else," Mary replied curtly, adding, "He works in a foundry and takes any manual work that offers him a decent wage from one week to the next. Like the rest of us in these times, he has to take what comes along. Beggars can't be choosers you know!"

"If this is as serious as it sounds to be, Mary, then you'd better bring your young man around for tea soon so we can give him a proper look over," her father said. "I just hope he's not too old for you, lass."

Mary could not believe her ears. She had been trying to keep Paddy her guilty secret for the best part of a year and now had to contend with her father wanting him to meet the family circus and even suggesting that Paddy take afternoon tea with them!

Later that day, Nancy and Mary's father approached the children hand in hand to announce some important news he felt they should be aware of, concerning himself and Nancy.

"Listen now!" Harry Lannon said as he looked at his family assembled before him. "I know that it hasn't yet been a year since your Ma passed away, yet, I know that she is looking down on all ten of you now, wishing you well. Nancy here and me ... what I mean to say is that given me and Nancy rub along well, and as she's now more or less part of the house fittings, we thought we'd better make everything proper and above board, so to speak. We've decided to get married next spring after a suitable period of mourning has passed for your dear mum. I know that Nancy loves you all, and it's our hope that you can all come to love and accept her as your new mother."

Upon hearing the news, Mary was the first to congratulate Nancy and dad. "I'm so pleased for you both" she said, "So, pleased."

That day proved to be one of the happiest in Mary's life. She immediately sat down and wrote Paddy a letter telling him about her father and Nancy's plans and about them wanting to meet him. Mary suggested that he try to get off from work early on her birthday of December 8th and catch the bus to Clonmel to meet up with her and her family. She said they would discuss the details next Sunday when they met up in Waterford as usual.

As Mary slept that night, she thought about her father's announcement of his spring marriage to Nancy. This sudden change in family dynamics affected Mary every bit as much as it affected any other family member, perhaps even more! With Nancy being prepared to take on her father as his new wife, Mary knew that this meant Nancy was willing to take on her nine siblings also!

For the first time in her life, everything Mary had ever wanted and dreamed of seemed possible; all was within her grasp. She slept more soundly and content that night than she had ever slept and the world outside appeared to be a much happier place to wake up to the following morning.

~~~

The next Sunday when Mary and Paddy met up, they stayed local to the centre of Waterford as they walked and talked like two animated teenagers planning next year's holidays. Fastened to the back of Paddy's bicycle was a small brown travelling suitcase.

After an hour or so, Paddy put his hand in his pocket and after extracting something, he showed Mary a ring. Looking at the plain gold band in Paddy's hand, Mary asked him, "What's that for?"

"Instead of walking around for four hours in the cold, Mary, or drinking pot after pot of tea, I thought … you know … I thought we would be cosier in a boarding house for the afternoon. I've got the money together to rent a room and we could pretend to be man and wife. We wouldn't have to stay overnight and could slip out quietly when it was time to catch your bus. What do think, Mary?"

At first, Mary felt like giving Paddy a piece of her mind for seeming to take her for granted, but then quickly relented, as she did not wish to spoil their day. Paddy retrieved the brown suitcase from the back of his bicycle and gave Mary the plain gold ring to put on her wedding finger.

Paddy knocked on the door of the first boarding house they passed which had a vacancy sign in the window. As they waited for the door to open, Mary stood anxiously behind him, partially hidden from view, as he addressed the property owner.

"We want a double room for the night,' Paddy said. 'Me and my wife."

The woman looked at Mary standing on the step below Paddy, and then after telling Paddy the price for the night, which he paid up front, she showed the couple to their room. As they climbed the steps and she spoke with Paddy, Mary felt the proprietor's eyes having a second suspicious look at her. It was at that moment when Mary realised that without a ring on her finger and at least one small suitcase purporting to carry overnight luggage, that entry to a double room in this boarding establishment would not have proved possible. It became apparent that Paddy had anticipated her acceptance all along.

During the next two hours, having engaged in as much foreplay as Mary would allow, the couple eventually made love. Mary had initially seemed more interested in cuddling and kissing than going the whole way, but then found herself giving in. They made love once that afternoon. While Paddy seemed highly satisfied to have gone all the way, Mary felt the experience to have been more mechanical as opposed to one of intimacy.

Having spoken of wedding plans earlier that afternoon with Paddy and having allowed herself to be taken by him, she now spiritually regarded her Kilkenny man as her husband in the eyes of God.

When Mary boarded the bus back to Clonmel later that day, she felt so happy with her life and future hopes. The next time they would meet would be on the evening of her eighteenth birthday when Paddy would visit her family home and join the rest of Mary's family in birthday celebrations.

Mary had been on the bus almost an hour when suddenly she realised that she still wore the thin gold ring upon her wedding finger. As she removed it and placed it inside her coat pocket, she smiled at the secret activities of her Sunday afternoon outing. She had started that afternoon to inwardly consider herself to be a woman in every sense.

Chapter Eight: '1911: A Year for Weddings'

The end of 1910 finished off well with Paddy's introduction to Mary's father and the rest of the family on the day of her eighteenth birthday.

Paddy was on his best behaviour and hit it off well with Mary's dad, Nancy and the rest of the family. Her father had a quiet word on the side with Paddy during the evening and seemed reassured after Paddy had confirmed his and Mary's intentions to marry in the near future. Forever the careful father, Harry Lannon seemed doubly reassured once he had ascertained that his daughter was not pregnant, saying, "Her mother always wanted a white wedding for all her girls and would turn in her grave, God Bless her, if she thought her eldest would be walking down the aisle in a veil of shame."

Once Mary accepted that Nancy was perfectly happy to take on the role of married woman again to a husband with a ready-made family of ten children, she and Paddy were able to plan for a future together. Before he cycled back home to Kilkenny that night, Paddy gave Mary a symbolic birthday present.

"I'm sorry I haven't been able to buy you a proper present before I get paid tomorrow, Mary," he said, "but I'd like you to have this as … a small token."

Mary looked at her present from Paddy. It was a small, holy patch with the image of St. Patrick. Paddy's mother had put the patch around his neck the day he had been born. As Paddy grew from infancy to child, the holy patch, which the priest who had baptised him wearing it had blessed, was fastened to the inside of his pram and placed inside his cot as he slept. When he grew older, Paddy never went anywhere without his patch inside his pocket. He considered the patch a talisman, which was one of the few things his mother had ever given him that he treasured. Had it been given to him by the pope himself, Paddy would not have prized it more highly than he already did, especially since his dear mother had died during his early teens, shortly followed by the death of his father from liver failure.

Mary recognised the importance of the patch in Paddy's life and list of humble possessions. She accepted it from Paddy gracefully and gently kissed him.

~~~

In May of 1911, Mary's father and Nancy got married. Nancy looked beautiful in her wedding dress and as her father walked up the aisle to stand alongside his bride to be, Mary could tell that her father had found a happiness in Nancy that neither he nor anyone else would have thought possible last year.

Afterwards, the doors to the family home were opened wide for anyone in the village to enter and greet the new bride and have tea and cake. In the evening, the local public house was filled to the rafters with boisterous revellers celebrating the good fortune of their friend and good neighbour, Harry Lannon, having found his one true love twice in a lifetime and marrying them both!

~~~

After her father had married Nancy, the already overcrowded family home held far too many bodies for Mary to continue living there. Within three weeks of her father's marriage to Nancy, Mary acquired lodgings in a house in Waterford. She also obtained regular work in a local Creamery on the Kilmeaden Road.

Her new lodgings meant that meeting Paddy would now be much easier and more often. No longer were the couple able to meet on Sunday afternoon only.

Paddy proved to be an arduous sweetheart and cycled across at least one evening during the week as well as every Sunday, with the occasional Saturday thrown in. While Mary wasn't officially allowed to have men in her room, the widow who owned the house always went out to play bridge in a Waterford Club for three hours every Sunday evening between 6pm and 9pm.

~~~

Mary's landlady was Prudence Cummins. She was an obsessive woman in her sixties who never varied her routine. Every single detail in her day was meticulously planned. Nothing was ever spontaneous with Prudence and it would have been unimaginable that she could have ever pleasingly entertained any man on the spur of a moment, let alone gratify her late husband's spontaneous advances in the bedroom! Mary and Paddy surmised that the poor man had been allowed 'it' (as Prudence called the act of sexual intercourse) on his birthday, at Christmas and if they ever managed to get away, at holiday time! On all other occasions, she would leave him to his own devices so long as he never expected her to watch or take part in the proceedings!

Prudence Cummins was a widow who religiously attended confession weekly. Apart from the sin of pride, she had nothing of substance to confess and took Holy Communion without fail every Sunday morning.

Prudence was both prude and proper in every way imaginable. She had only been prepared to take Mary in as a lodger, after ascertaining she was a good Catholic who attended confession, church and communion with the regularity of a nun.

Indeed, despite there being a number of Catholic churches to attend in Waterford, and most of them closer than the one she attended weekly, Prudence Cummins would attend none other than 'Waterford Cathedral, The Cathedral of the Most Holy Trinity.' Only the Cathedral was good enough for this high minded Catholic of lofty station; this holy woman who was patiently living out the remainder of her existence on earth before taking up her rightful place in heaven.

John Roberts had built the cathedral in 1793 and Prudence would never consider the dwelling being worthy of mention without reminding the listener that the building was 'Ireland's oldest Catholic Cathedral'.

Over the next three months, on a Sunday evening, Paddy and Mary would sneak into her bedroom for a kiss and a cuddle after Prudence Cummins had gone off to her bridge club. Mary got Paddy to agree that they would not make love again before their wedding night, as she wanted to walk down the aisle without child inside her.

Deep down, Mary had always believed that a man and woman should not have sexual relations before their wedding night. She viewed the act as being there for the prime purpose to procreate life instead of solely to satisfy man's lust. Poor Paddy never knew the pig in a poke he was taking on the day he married Mary Lannon

~~~

Paddy and Mary had put as much money away as they possibly could to save for their wedding and they planned to marry on Mary's nineteenth birthday, which fell on Friday, December 8th, 1911.

The couple knew that they were not in the market to own their own house; such were not the dreams of ordinary folk. The best they could ever hope for was to find a rented property without a leaking roof and with an understanding property owner.

Over the coming months, Mary and Paddy used their spare time looking for rented properties around the Waterford and Kilmeaden area. They eventually heard of a terraced cottage with two bedrooms in a village three miles farther on from Kilmeaden where Mary worked. The village was Portlaw and the elected cottage was due to become vacant to rent in late November when the present occupiers moved out to live and work in Connemara.

The following week, Mary and Paddy travelled into Portlaw to check out the cottage. While there, Paddy looked up the proprietor to 14, William Street as well as arrange a viewing of the property with Mary.

As Paddy sought out the proprietor of the cottage, Mary remained outside it for his return. Being the early 1900s, it was still regarded as being unseemly for the women folk to do business with their men folk, especially unmarried ones!

Paddy found the property owner in the local pub where he usually spent all Sunday between noon and closing time. After a few pints and a lengthy chat, Paddy and the owner came to a gentleman's agreement and sealed the paperless contract with the exchange of spitted palms. An agreed rent was established between the two men, with the first week's rent to fall due on the 26th November.

Paddy and Mary looked the property over and satisfied themselves it was suitable to start a family besides being within their means to rent.

~~~

On December 8th, Paddy and Mary got married in the Catholic Church in Portlaw. Having starting their married life in the Parish of Portlaw, they only considered it fitting that they should get married there, have their first child baptised there, make their children's First Holy Communion there and also have them confirmed there.

Mary looked lovely at the wedding, even though the couple had not enough money to buy a traditional bridal dress. Her dress of white satin had been made by a 'seamstress' in Clonmel; or to be more precise, a thirty-year-old woman with sewing skills who worked in the post office there, but who had a flare for fashion since childhood and who had always dreamed of becoming a seamstress.

Despite their house being sparse in furniture, it held the essentials of table, chairs, bed and crockery. Paddy and Mary were over the moon to be starting a life together, which no longer required them hiding and skulking whenever they wanted to be alone.

Paddy got himself a job in the 'Portlaw Spinning Company' as a general maintenance man and though the money was minimal unless overtime hours were available, the job was relatively easy and overall, stress free.

~~~

Their first two years of marriage were not easy times for Paddy to readjust to, but for Mary, they were undoubtedly the happiest two years she had yet known. Love making to Patrick was synonymous with the act of baby making to Mary and the frequency of thrice weekly was all she could bring her body to bear. Any spare money the couple managed to put aside would be saved in a box in their bedroom for their first-born.

Mary should now have been approaching the zenith of her dreams, the starting of her very own family, but instead, she was to suffer month after month of bitter disappointment.

For over three years, Mary and Paddy tried to produce a child. Each month, Mary continued to see signs of her usual menstrual period as if its presence represented a symbolic sign of punishment from God for having copulated before her marriage! She saw her own spilled blood no differently to that of the blood of Christ, as just one more nail in her cross!

Paddy was the more patient and reassuring of the two marriage partners and used to say, "Don't worry, Mary. The babies shall come when they come; just you be ready!"

Mary could not wait though. She had waited all of her life to give birth to a baby and had even given her body three times weekly to Paddy during their first three years of their marriage in order to have a child of her own.

Whenever the couple visited her father, stepmother Nancy and Mary's siblings in Clonmel, both father and Nancy would ask when they would be hearing the patter of little feet in 14, William Street. After three years of asking though, they asked no more, recognising that the mere mentioning of the absence of children wounded Mary to the quick.

Chapter Nine: 'Marriage Breakup'

For over three years, Mary and Paddy tried to have children, but alas, none came. Mary eventually drummed up the courage to ask her husband to get himself tested with her. She suggested that they were tested in Waterford to see if both were able to have children. This suggestion of Mary's caused their very first big argument.

Paddy was essentially too proud ever to contemplate that he might not be able to give Mary children and considered it unmanly with the suggestion were he to discover that he was firing blanks in the bedroom. Mary, on the other hand, considered the issue too grave not to find out why children had evaded them for so long now.

After numerous rows, the issue started to sour their previously happy relationship so much, that reluctantly, Paddy agreed. The tests confirmed that while one of the married couple could have a child, the other could not!

Blood tests revealed that Paddy was infertile. Reasons forwarded included his condition of diabetes since childhood plus a hernia in his groin. Another possible reason was Paddy having been exposed to lead poisoning at the age of eight years old from a public-shared lavatory that four neighbouring families used in Kilkenny.

Paddy found the news very hard to accept and though he hardly drank alcohol prior to his marriage, he soon abandoned his abstinence. For the following six months, Paddy would arrive home too often the worse for wear, having spent a few hours in the pub after leaving work.

The deterioration in their relationship was so rapid that most contact between them now seemed cold and loveless. As far as Mary was concerned, there was no point in them making love any more, as it was a futile gesture that brought her no pleasure. After Paddy learned he was infertile, his sexual interest also waned and before long, he started to lose the very gentleness in his ways. Such gentleness had been the very trait which had attracted Mary to him in the first place!

The couple gradually stopped talking and eating together and it was only after they had stopped sleeping together in the same bed that Paddy realised he was no longer a good-enough man for the woman he had married. The sudden change in their relationship had appeared as quickly as any mountain accident. It was as if an avalanche had swept into their marriage and had buried any trace of happiness, which had once existed between them, beneath a mountain of snow.

All joint visits to Mary's father and family in Clonmel ceased and on the few occasions Mary now saw them, she was always alone. Naturally, they would enquire where Paddy was and Mary would usually provide some excuse regarding his absence, which eventually became less convincing the more times she made one!

On one occasion, Nancy took Mary to one side and after a brief time together; Mary broke her silence and told her stepmother about the deterioration in her marriage and the reasons for such. While Nancy obviously sympathised with Mary's plight, she also urged Mary not to write Paddy off too soon as she was convinced he was a good man. Nancy intrinsically felt that it was only natural for Paddy to feel bad that he would never be able to be a father in more than name and that the mere shock of him discovering that he could not give his wife a child would be enough to make any man feel unsure of himself ever again!

After that conversation with Nancy, Mary felt guilty. She returned to Portlaw determined to try again with her husband Paddy and to restore, if possible, the closeness they once felt for each other. She resolved that if they could even become 'best friends', that might be enough of itself to keep them together, enabling the passage of time to lead to a more peaceful resolution between them.

While Paddy was pleased to find a semblance of peace return to their failing marriage, things were never quite the same between the couple as they had once been. A cautious truce was established, which recognised the roles of each partner within the household. Every time the couple's eyes met however, each knew that their relationship had crossed their Rubicon. Their marital relationship had crossed their river of regret, and both knew there would be no going back to the happy and loving relationship they had once shared when first married and dreaming of family to come.

Another year passed between the couple, but despite their honest attempt to salvage their marriage, no improvement in their relationship proved sustainable. Mary seemed to become more and more depressed with her motherless status, Paddy drowned his sorrows in the pub most evenings and remained out late. The couple gradually drew farther apart and eventually; neither seemed to possess the will any longer to stop the widening separation.

~~~

One evening while waiting for the bus to take her back from the Creamery in Kilmeaden after her day's work had finished, it started to rain heavily. As Mary cowered from the pelting rain with a handkerchief over her hair to offer some little protection, Sean Morris, the Supervisor at Mary's place of works, joined her at the bus stop.

Seeing Mary get a good soaking in the rain led Sean to offer her his coat. Of course, Mary refused, but Sean would hear no argument and continued taking it from his own back and draping it across the shoulders of Mary.

Sean lived seven miles farther on from the Portlaw bus stop where Mary alighted, in a small cottage on the road into Carrick-on-Suir. He had never married and seemed more interested in remaining single while he advanced his career at the Creamery. It was rumoured by the women at the Creamery that Sean was a man with an eye for the women, so long as they were single, attractive and were prepared to remain emotionally unattached.

Sean earned a good wage as Supervisor at the Creamery and he wanted no demands by another that might hamper his career. Sean knew that if he played his cards right and avoided any manner of trouble that might tarnish his reputation, it was rumoured that he would naturally advance to the role of manager of the Creamery when the present manager retired in six years' time. Being a manager before he was barely thirty years old was unheard of and so Sean was as keen as mustard to protect his image and reputation.

While Sean had frequently caught the same bus as that of Mary after finishing work, whenever additional business did not keep him behind, he had never sat with her previously. It was not until after that afternoon in the rain when he had behaved like a chivalrous knight and had given Mary his coat that he started to view her in a different light and started sitting alongside her on the bus whenever they caught it on their way home together.

Having looked closely at Mary that day in the rain and having seen her wet clothes make the outline of her breasts more fulsome, had stirred a passion in him for this Portlaw woman, which had not previously existed.

As fate decrees, those who seek it not, sometimes find, but not to expect it at all is one sure way of having it fall into one's lap!

Within a short space of time, Mary and her Supervisor Sean had crossed the divide from that of admirer to one of greater intimacy. That which had started as a harmless gesture by a rainy bus stop, gradually grew into the development of a closeness between the couple, followed by the 'chance meetings' they might have in Waterford where a cup of tea and a chat might be had over flirtatious chatter and naughty thoughts.

~~~

The first time Mary and Sean had sex was to be the only time they slept together. It happened when Mary's husband Paddy incurred an accident and was in hospital for the week with a badly broken leg. Mary told Sean she would be visiting her husband that evening in hospital and they agreed to meet up afterwards by the clock on the quayside.

As Mary waited for Sean as arranged beneath the clock tower, she thought about all those happier times when she had met her husband Paddy there during their courtship days. A large part of her felt guilty about being a married woman and secretly meeting another man in clandestine circumstances, especially when her husband was laid up in hospital, while a bit of her was simply bursting to feel alive again. She needed to feel wanted again by someone; anyone!

Shortly after Mary and Sean met up, he indicated his fear of being seen in public, outside work hours, especially with a married woman by any of the Creamery workers. He feared damage to his reputation if he and Mary were to become the topic of salacious gossip in their work place.

He suggested to Mary to come back to his cottage with him on the Carrick-on-Suir road for the night. Not being the kind of woman that any man could persuade if she did not want persuading, Mary surprised Sean and herself and agreed to sleep overnight at the cottage.

It had been a long time since Mary had experienced sex with her husband Paddy and their exclusivity had often made her wonder in the last year, what it might be like with another man. Paddy was the only man she had ever slept with, and part of her was curious as to how having sex with Sean would compare.

She was sad to find the experience highly disappointing. Her encounter with Sean no more satisfying than her experience with Paddy had been. Indeed, in some ways, it was far worse. It was more painful and much more degrading in after effects.

Sean did not display the gentleness and consideration, which her husband Paddy did. There was little foreplay and no time to waste as far as Sean was concerned and he employed a mechanical process that he had reduced to three quick moves before obtaining checkmate. His three moves of seduction included getting her undressed, getting it in and getting it off as fast and as roughly as he could!

This illicit nightly stopover provided Mary with more shame than she had ever felt before. The following day, she had the day off work pretending to be sick. She had plenty of time to think about what had happened and after having had time to dwell on her actions, an avalanche of Catholic guilt descended to curse her infidelity.

When Mary next saw Sean at work, she cornered him later in the morning and indicated she was ending their relationship before it went any farther and destroyed both their lives. Mary told him, "Sorry, Sean, but it has been a ghastly mistake, a 'one off' that should never have happened. It won't be happening again. Sorry."

To her surprise, Sean seemed extremely relieved at her decision and indicated his agreement saying that he was sure she was right. In truth, Sean had found his sexual encounter with Mary to be more of an anti-climax than he had ever envisaged and even less sexually pleasurable than what he could have achieved in a night of his own company! He believed Mary to be a cold fish out of water with whichever man she found herself in bed!

~~~

Mary's unhappy marriage to Paddy continued until the last quarter of 1915 when Paddy packed his case and left her for good. It was the 4th October when Paddy left Mary.

While the couple had tried to rub along against any odds of success over the previous year, the situation became untenable for either party to continue their sham of a marriage once it became clear that Mary was pregnant. This pregnant state of his wife told Paddy that she had been unfaithful to their marriage vows and left Mary being unable to deny it, even had she wanted to!

Paradoxically, Mary was only partly shocked to discover that she was with child to another man outside her marriage. Contrary to her predicament, another part of her produced thoughts of anticipated pleasure to come by giving birth to her very own child.

Indeed, Mary even started to wonder if she had unconsciously engineered the situation of her night out with Sean that had led to her impregnation and subsequent pregnancy. Thinking back upon the occasion, she recalled that during the height of his sexual arousal, where the point of no return approached, she made no move or spoke no word that would lead to his withdrawal and the spilling of his seed outside her.

Of course, she could not tell Paddy or anyone else for that matter who the father was, and as for Sean, she resolved that he would never learn of the produce of their brief encounter in Carrick-on Suir.

Mary had decided to bring up their child on her own from day one of learning she was pregnant. She did not need any man to support her or the child. All of her life she had been the support to other children and finally. Now, it would be to her own child whom she would mother!

~~~

After finding out about his wife's unfaithfulness and not wishing to be gossiped about as having been 'the cuckold husband', Paddy kept Mary's sordid secret and simply left her to come up with any required explanations to her Portlaw neighbours of his absence.

Mary needed a plausible tale to satisfy the curiosity of her neighbours after her husband Paddy had left their marital home to seek work in England, saying that he would never see her again and advising her of the futility of ever pressing him for any financial support to bring up another man's bastard.

Mary quickly formulated her plans almost as soon as her husband Paddy had left her. She told the neighbours that Paddy had gone to seek work and better prospects in England and that she and the baby would eventually be joining them there when the bairn was old enough to travel.

Mary had already decided that she would not be hanging around Portlaw one day longer than she needed to after her child had been born. She did not intend to give the gossips and 'holier than thou' neighbours a stick to beat her with for the rest of her life whenever a falling out was had, should they ever discover her secret. No way did she intend to raise their suspicions or risk them finding out that the child was not her husband's bairn. She did not intend to ever hear the malicious whisper of another call her innocent child, 'Bastard!'

A few months after the birth, Mary decided to leave Portlaw; ostensibly, to join her husband in England where they would start afresh.

Chapter Ten: 'Mary's Motherhood'

Two months into her pregnancy, Mary got the scare of her life when her first medical examination revealed that she was expecting not one child, but twins, or to be more precise, two sets of twins!

"Four!" Mary exclaimed in disbelief upon hearing the news.

"Yes, the examination shows there to be four foetuses," the hospital consultant replied. "It looks like quads, Mrs Fanning."

"Talk about waiting for a baby for the whole of one's life and just when it seems none will ever come, along come four, all at once," Mary mused to herself.

Three days after hearing the news of her multiple pregnancy, Mary handed in her notice at the Kilmeaden Creamery and told the Supervisor Sean and the rest of her working colleagues that she would soon be joining her husband Paddy in England. She kept completely quiet about her pregnant state, as she had not yet started to show her condition and wanted to avoid any unnecessary gossip for as long as possible.

Mary knew that this was something she would be unable to hide from her father, Nancy and her siblings once she had given birth. Mary wrote to Nancy and requested that she visit her alone in Portlaw, indicating she had some news to tell her. Mary wanted to use Nancy as an intermediary, to break the news to her father.

The following week, Nancy called to see Mary at the Portlaw address. Mary told Nancy everything there was to tell, including her single act of adultery, without identifying the father of her children to be!

While being naturally shocked by Mary's news, Nancy agreed to break it to her father and agreed to visit her weekly during the months ahead. Nancy acted more like a best friend to Mary as opposed to a mother figure and never once did she utter any words of reproof against her stepdaughter.

While her father was naturally shocked when Nancy told him of his daughter's adultery and her pregnant state, he nevertheless would not abandon her. He agreed to pay Mary's landlord in Portlaw the rent for her property until she gave up the tenancy.

~~~

Three months into Mary's pregnancy, further examinations by the doctor revealed that not all was well. Two of the foetuses had not survived. It would seem that each set of twins were sharing a placenta that greatly increased the risk of a co-twin demise, and one of the foetuses from each twin set had already perished inside Mary's womb.

Mary learned that when the twins are identical and share a placenta, there is an increased risk that the other twin will also pass away. This is for two reasons: first, they share all their genes. Mary learned the underlying reasons why the first foetus passed away from each twin set might have been a genetic syndrome or another genetic risk factor that the identical twin also possessed. Second, sharing a placenta with a demised twin invariably leads to anaemia, low blood pressure, and restriction of blood flow to the living twin, which can result in death. Mary learned that because of the increased risk of neurological impairments in the surviving twin members, doctors would have to be prepared to deliver the remaining two babies around the thirty-two-week gestation period if they were to have an increased chance of surviving.

Poor Mary heard this sad news all on her own. Two of her unborn babies had already died inside her and the other two also risked death before birth. Mary became overwrought with grief and went to her bed for four days without rising, apart from urinating.

When Nancy next visited Portlaw, she found Mary deeply depressed. She phoned word via the Portlaw Post Office and the Post Office in Clonmel and asked that a message be passed to her husband, informing him that his daughter Mary was not well and that his wife would be staying the next week with her until she was back on her feet.

When Nancy heard the latest news regarding the death of two of her planned children and the risk to life of the remaining two, it became apparent what had depressed poor Mary so. Mary told her that they would have to perform a caesarean around the thirty-two-week stage of her pregnancy and until then, she would have to carry two live and two dead babies inside her!

Far from it being the happiest occasion that Mary had dreamed it would be ever since her childhood years, all she had to look forward to with certainty was the delivery of two dead babies without knowing if the other two would survive!

After one week's presence of her stepmother in the house, Mary gradually improved. She had previously stopped eating altogether and only just started having a small bowl of soup again or a baked potato after Nancy had told her that there was simply no chance of the other two babies surviving until delivery unless she took some nourishment!

Nancy urged the mother to be, "If you won't eat for yourself, then at least eat for the two babies you are carrying!"

Nancy returned to Clonmel. She needed to restore some order to her own house before returning to stay with Mary again for as long as possible. Over the next three months, Nancy managed to stay over in Portlaw with her stepdaughter Mary for half of each week; returning to Clonmel to fend for her husband and the nine children for the remaining three days of the week.

~~~

After Mary had given birth, Nancy stayed a week at her Portlaw home for the family funeral of the two children who never made it. While Mary attended their funeral, along with a few nosey neighbours who insisted on standing by the graveside to offer the grieving mother their support, Nancy looked after the newborn infants Nellie and Nora inside 14, William Street, Portlaw.

As with most funeral days, sod's law prevailed and the atrocious weather added to the gloom of the occasion. It started raining heavily before it poured down and soaked anyone who stood around the graveside.

As Mary saw the extremely small coffins, which were no larger than sewing boxes, lowered into the burial plot, she found it impossible to contain her grief. Each tiny coffin bore on its surface the carved names Mary had given her dead babies. She had named them Nancy and Maureen, after her two mothers. Mary's heart had been broken in two and she let out an outpouring of tears, the like of which had never been seen at the edge of any Portlaw graveside before that day or since.

There was one particular moment as Mary looked down at the small coffins that she felt like falling into the grave opening with them, so that her two small mites would not feel alone in the darkness of the cold earth.

It also pained Mary that neither child had been given the sacrament of baptism, having died in her womb. Had they been born alive, even though they might have lived but mere minutes, the priest on hand would have baptised them and prevented their enforced stay in purgatory.

Two weeks later, Mary, Nancy, and the two babies, Nellie and Nora returned to the family home in Clonmel. Tenancy of the rented house at 14, William Street was duly relinquished.

The people of Portlaw had been informed that Mary and her two babies would be spending a brief period with her father and siblings in Clonmel before travelling across the sea to England, where they would meet up with her husband Paddy, the children's father.

~~~

Mary and the two babies lived at her father's house for almost three months before she decided that it was time to strike out on her own in England.

When Harry Lannon learned that the children's father was an unmarried man who knew not of the birth of his two children, he could not accept that his daughter had been morally right to keep this vital information from the natural father. From what his wife Nancy had told him, neither party had proved innocent in their illicit coupling. Both had knowingly slept together without any need of enticement, persuasion or protection!

Harry Lannon also found it impossible to speak to his eldest daughter about her adultery with another man, and inwardly, he did not blame Paddy Fanning for leaving Mary high and dry after he had eventually found out about her infidelity and its consequences! In fact, Nancy's dad told her one night in no uncertain words, that had her mother or his wife Nancy ever done that to him, he would have packed his suitcase and left her to fend on her own also, whether she had one bairn to look after or ten!

Mary knew her father's views on the matter and respected them by not once voicing her own in defence of her actions. Besides, Mary knew deep down that her father spoke only the truth; no more and no less than the simple facts of the matter. Mary knew that she had done her husband wrong and part of her believed that the death of two of her unborn children had been God's punishment for her adulterous behaviour.

Chapter Eleven: 'Liverpool: August, 1916'

Three months after arriving back at her father's house, Mary and her two infants travelled to Dublin to catch the ferry across the Irish Sea to Liverpool. Nancy accompanied them to Dublin in order to see them set sail safely.

As Mary left her family abode, her father embraced her without saying a word and turned away to prevent her seeing his silent tears streaming down his cheeks. Mary left, not knowing that she would never see him alive again.

Nancy travelled to Dublin by train with Mary and the infants and saw them safely onto the ferry. Mary cried bitterly as Nancy waved them off and for the first time in her life, she felt very alone and without any support.

She started to fear the fact that she would step off the ferry with two small children and just over seven pounds and a few shillings in her purse, knowing just one person who might be in England; her husband Paddy!

It was August 3rd, 1916 when Mary Fanning and her infants landed off the ferry in Liverpool docks. The weather was warm and having no pram with her, Mary carried Nellie and Nora, snuggly wrapped and placed inside a large woven hand basket.

It was eleven in the morning and as Mary left the quayside, she had never seen so many busy people in one place before. All around her, she could hear the hustle and bustle of Liverpool workers waking up for the day. On one side, she heard the noise of ship pulleys hoisting cargo off and onto the many ships that transported food and other merchandise across the sea.

As she walked off the quayside towards the more populated part of the city, Mary could still hear the life of the docks loud in her ears as workers' clogs clanked their footsteps on the wooden flooring of the harboured sailing vessels as they went about their daily work.

"Penny for a cuppa, Misses," a young boy aged around ten years old said to Mary as he tugged on her coat.

Mary looked upon the boy and seeing his heart-wrenching look, she immediately took pity on him and went to open her purse, which she had concealed in her child basket, beneath the covering of her infants. The boy had pleading eyes of innocent blue placed within the centre of his mucky and grimy face. He held his hand outright as a silent plea to Mary's generosity and Mary placed a thru-penny bit in it. The boy smiled and flung his arms around Mary in an embrace of gratitude as he profusely replied, "Thank you, kind lady, oh thank you, thank you!"

Then the beggar boy smiled at Mary and asked to see the lovely babes, a request that Mary thought harmless, so obliged. The boy looked closely at the infants in their basket, then returned to Mary, and started hugging her in appreciation again.

It seemed that minutes passed by before Mary was able to get the street urchin to withdraw his hugging arms from around her waist. The boy left, continuing to thank Mary profusely for her generosity as he walked away.

~~~

Over the next four hours, Mary searched high and low for some suitable accommodation for herself and babies, but each place she tried, refused to accommodate women on their own and particularly, an unaccompanied woman with a child. The notices in most house windows that put up boarders frequently stated 'No Irish, No Blacks, No Prostitutes, No Dogs, No Children, and No Single Women!'

As she read these lists of undesirables in the windows of the boarding houses, Mary started to think that were she ever to find a place to stay in Liverpool, she knew in advance the type of other guests she'd find staying there alongside her; white English men of single status!

It had started to grow cooler as evening approached. Mary had not eaten since yesterday or so much as had a cup of tea since she had stepped off the boat, and she needed to find a roof for the night. The only break she had taken all day had been to breast feed the two infants twice in the public shelter of a bus stop.

It was six pm when Mary, by now weary and close to exhaustion, walked up the three steps of number 33, Silk Street and rapped the metal doorknocker which was fashioned in the shape of a lion. As Mary awaited another rejection by the property owner, her stomach rumbled with lack of food.

The door opened and Mary made her request with eyes cast down, as if awaiting an immediate refusal, accompanied by the usual excuses she had heard trotted out all day.

Just then, one her babies stared to cry and the crying of one got the other one crying also. "Shit!" thought Mary as she lifted her eyes to meet the property owner looking back at her.

"I arrived from Ireland this morning off the ferry with my two infants," Mary said, adding, "and I need a place to stay. I can pay the rent for a week in advance. We will be moving inland to meet my husband Paddy next week in Wakefield. He came over to England six months ago and hasn't seen his children yet."

The proprietor was Doris Storey. Doris was in her mid-twenties and gave Mary the once over before replying, "I have a small attic room if that would suit you and the children which you can have for £5.10 shillings per week, up front. It's not big, but is very clean and is large enough for you and your bairns…and if they cry during the night, none of the other three lodgers on the floor below will hear them."

Mary was so relieved not to be turned away again and went to get her purse and pay the rent. Mary placed her hand beneath the children's blanket cover, but felt nothing there, apart from the tiny foot of one of her infants. Lifting the cover up, she saw that her purse had vanished. It had gone! Suddenly, Mary remembered the street urchin who had begged the price of a cup of tea off her earlier that morning and his hugs of lengthy gratitude and close inspection of her daughters in their Moses basket.

"He robbed me!" Mary exclaimed. "The little shit robbed me!" she said as she started to cry.

Having at last found a place to stay, she no longer had the means to stay there! Turning around in tears, Mary thanked the proprietor and started to leave.

"Come back," the proprietor replied to Mary as she started to walk away down Silk Street. "Come back here now with those two little bairns."

"You can stop the night and in the light of morning we'll decide what's to be done. Never let it be said that Doris Storey had it in her heart to turn away a mother and two small infants from her door back onto the streets of Liverpool at night for want of a few shillings when there's an attic going spare!" Doris said to Mary as she ushered her inside the house.

Mary thanked Doris profusely. About half an hour later, Mary had settled down in the attic room and was breastfeeding both infants when she heard a knock on her room door. Before she could get up, Doris opened the door and entered. She was carrying a warm mug of tea and a plate of spam sandwiches.

"After you've fed the bairns you can feed yourself. You'll sleep a lot better on a fuller stomach, dear," the kind host said.

The following morning, Doris offered Mary breakfast in her downstairs living quarters. As Mary ate a few slices of toast and a boiled egg, she placed her two children on the floor beside her in their Moses basket.

Doris came back in the room with a second pot of tea, a cup for herself to drink from and sat down at the breakfast table to talk to her unpaying lodger.

"Now then….." Doris started to say before searching for a name with which to address Mary.

"Mary, my name's Mary Fanning," Mary replied, "and these two young ladies in the basket are Nellie and Nora, aged four months."

Before Mary would allow herself to impose farther upon the good wishes of the proprietor who had already been too kind to her, she needed to set the record straight and come clean about her real circumstances.

"Before you say another word," Mary said, 'I need to come clean with you. I wasn't entirely honest with you yesterday on your doorstep. Yes, I did have my purse stolen and my husband Paddy is in England … but …. he's not the father of my children and I haven't the slightest intention of meeting up with him ever again, since he walked out on me over a year ago!"

"Nay, lass," Doris replied, "You're not the first unaccompanied woman to turn up on my doorstep with children in tow and you'll not be the last. I don't know where my man Patrick is at this precise moment, as I haven't heard from him in over six months now. He could be prisoner to the Germans or even dead in a ditch in the corner of some muddy trench in a Flanders field. But, I'll tell you this, Mary Fanning from Ireland; if he is standing at the doorstep of some French farmhouse on a cold and lonely night, hungry and wounded and in need of shelter, I pray that the householder is Christian enough to recognise his plight and will not turn him in to the enemy or away from her door empty handed! My mother always said, 'What goes round comes around!'"

Over the next two hours, Mary and Doris talked and by the time they had done talking, Mary knew she had been come into contact with one of God's earthly angels and felt less anxious than she'd been since she had boarded the ferry in Dublin, bound for England.

Both women, having been born within a few years of each other, found conversation easy and in some respects, they had much in common. Mary did wonder though how one so young could have managed to have acquired so large a house and a steady income stream.

Doris agreed to put her and the children up and to look after the infants during the day as soon as Mary started feeding them by bottle instead of breast. This would allow Mary the opportunity to pursue some work. Doris indicated there would be no additional weekly charge for this babysitting service, as being childless and always having wanted children, she would consider it a pleasure to look after the two girls in their mother's absence. As regarding the payment of their rent, until she started to earn, Doris agreed to let Mary work it off at the boarding house washing, ironing, and generally helping in whatever area of work needed doing to keep the establishment running smoothly.

Chapter Twelve: 'The War Years'

The war between England and Germany had been ongoing for almost two years by the time Mary and her daughters had started to live in Liverpool, and though food rationing had not fully arrived yet, part rationing was slowly creeping in, making certain products harder to come by.

With their men in uniform fighting the Germans in Europe, the war years provided ample work for female civilians on the home front. Much of the work though was limited in scope. Many women in Liverpool remained determined to do their bit for England so that the country could emerge victorious over the Hun and provide a land fit to live in, where freedom of speech and freedom from want was the entitlement of all.

It was widely said that this war would be a war to end all wars and the way that many women contributed to the war effort was by working in the munition and other factories across Merseyside and in all the other cities of the nation.

This war was the first truly mechanised war and needed men, women, machines, ships, planes, submarines, cruisers, destroyers, merchant vessels, tanks and an ample supply of munitions to help fight it. Millions of shells rained down from the heavens on both sides and dozens of munition factories in

Liverpool were required to keep supplies heading to the front lines.

Liverpool was home to eight munition factories, which operated round the clock. Approximately 80% women staffed these factories. Factories supplying the soldiers were located in Edge Lane, the Cunard works at Primrose Road, North Haymarket, Lambert Road Tramway Depot, Aintree National Filling Factory, Clyde Street, Brasenose Road in Bootle and the Litherland Explosives Factory.

It was dangerous work in the munition factories and women sometimes died of poisoning from the chemicals used to make weaponry, along with other workplace injuries such as accidental explosions. Whatever the rest of the country did towards the war effort, Liverpool and its men and women most certainly did their bit to pull their weight in the nation's battle!

~~~

Over the next eight months, Mary and her two children settled into life at the home of Doris Storey. It took Mary around three weeks after placing her babies on the bottle before she felt reassured enough to seek work; leaving Doris to look after the girls in her absence.

Once Mary had started her search for work, it became evident that she would find it much easier were she to get a job in one of the munition factories. Within two days of applying for a job, 'The Litherland Explosives Factory', which made bullets and tank shells, eventually employed her.

With regard to the supervision of her two girls in her absence, Doris never seemed to see her daily charge of them as being a chore. In many ways, she loved doing things for the girls and looking after them gave her a feeling of immense pleasure and satisfaction. This role made her a mother substitute in the absence of their natural mother, but it also provided the childless Doris with the opportunity to exercise her own maternal instincts; instincts which had laid dormant for far too long and welcomed satisfying.

Without knowing it at the time of their first meeting, Mary and Doris was to share far more in common with each other than they could ever have imagined.

Doris and her army husband Patrick had only been wed two years, and before they'd had sufficient time to settle down to experiencing life as a married couple, war was declared. Within the month, Patrick received his call up papers.

With regard to the bedroom side of their union, this had never been as satisfactory as it ought to have been between man and wife. Doris undoubtedly loved her husband to bits, but sexually they never quite hit it off. Doris knew deep down that their sexual incompatibility was an issue that would need addressing when Patrick eventually returned from war, were their marriage ever to thrive.

~~~

By the time Christmas, 1917 arrived at 33, Silk Street, Doris, Mary and the two small sisters operated more like a closely-knit family unit as opposed to a relationship between benevolent proprietor and grateful lodger and mother of two.

Never once, did Doris complain about supervising the girls during Mary's absence at work and within a short space of time, Mary and the girls had all their meals in the privacy of Doris' private part of the house on the ground floor. Indeed, the only time they spent in their own room was at night-time when they slept.

Within a matter of months, Mary no longer felt anxious at the start of her factory shift when she left the children with her friend Doris for the day. She knew that they would be loved and well cared for in her absence.

As for Doris, she enjoyed having Mary and the girls living with her. Since her husband Patrick had gone off to war, she had only seen him once. This had been after him being granted a 48-hour pass, when he surprisingly returned home one weekend on leave. Doris was over the moon to see him, but worried so much about Patrick when the time came for him to return to the front line.

She told Mary, "The change in Patrick was great …. not so much how he looked, though he was much gaunter, but more how he acted, not just around me, but anyone he met that weekend. Try as I may to get him to tell me what it was like being at the front; he just refused to say, apart from muttering that I could never understand. He said that no one back home could ever understand, as we'd have to have been there to know what it was really like!"

"I suppose there are things men have to do in war that shames them in peace time when they think upon it?" Mary replied sympathetically.

"I know," Doris said, "but I sometimes think they forget that it's hard back on the home front also; it's hard not knowing if our loved ones are alive or dead, captured by the enemy, wounded or abandoned in some deserted ditch. If there's a hardness to be had in it all, Mary, it lies in the 'not knowing' that is hardest of all! 'Not knowing' how the battle is really going and whether or not the news that the radio speaks is true or merely government propaganda. 'Not knowing' if the food we have in the larder today will last the week out, and 'not knowing' if the Zeppelins' night time bombs will land on us in our beds. 'Not knowing' if the telegraph boy who comes down the street with his official telegrams in their sinister brown envelopes indicating that a son, brother or husband has died or has gone missing in action will stop at your door, or the door of your neighbours with the heart-breaking news you have long feared, but dare not voice! All this 'not knowing', Mary, is driving me mad!"

Doris started to cry. It was the first time that Mary had seen her cry and it pained to see her friend weep. Mary put her arms around Doris and wiped her eyes, kissing her gently as she did. Doris just held on tight, as if to make a magic moment last a few seconds longer.

Doris had openly cried with the thought of her husband's possible death and the voicing of all her uncertainties of 'not knowing.' What had really made her tears harder to express however, was the hidden guilt each teardrop secretly contained.

Doris loved her husband and had greatly missed him once he went to war. She had constantly worried about his possible whereabouts, fearing his capture by the enemy. When asleep, she frequently dreamt of him lying injured in the battle trenches or even dying on foreign soil, having been gunned down by the enemy or blown to bits by a mortar shell!

Ever since Mary and the children had come into her life however, a part of Doris, which she tried to suppress, was happy that Patrick was not here with her now. Had he been so, Doris knew that his presence, while producing immense relief, would spoil her pleasure. Part of her made her both fear his death on the battlefront, but reluctantly welcome the status of 'widowhood' that would inevitably follow such loss!

This was the greatest of all ironies and it plagued Doris immeasurably, making her as guilty as any wife had ever been who had dared to consider in her most secret of thoughts, the death of a good man as 'a way out!'

Doris had to reconcile herself with the knowledge that her husband Patrick made her happiest by his absence, while it was Mary and her daughters who were now wholly responsible for making her happy to wake up each morning and face the day ahead!

~~~

Later that month, one evening after Mary had returned from her factory shift and the girls had been put to bed for the night, Doris started talking to Mary about her upbringing.

Mary learned that Doris had been an only child who had experienced doting parents throughout her childhood. In many ways, Doris had lived a sheltered existence. Her father in particular, though loving, was reportedly a strict man who managed Doris' life from the start to the end of each day.

Doris' dad had worked as an accountant with one of the law firms in the city for most of his life and received a good enough level of remuneration to make him salaried and of middle class status. The family never wanted for anything material and any spare money her father had, he used to buy stocks and shares.

Doris was strongly discouraged from mixing with other children during her early childhood years, most of whom whose lifestyles and background circumstances, her father disapproved. Overall, Reginald Nuttall believed other children to represent the threat of being a bad influence on his daughter. Doris always had to return home from school within half an hour of finishing her lessons for the day; and having a brief stopover at a friend's house on the way home was strictly forbidden.

Mary learned that while Doris seemed to have adapted to her lifestyle, never having known any other way, she nevertheless resented the many restrictions her father placed on her freedoms, particularly when she entered her mid-teens. Her father always wanted to know every little thing about her from one minute to the next; where she was when she was not with them, what she was doing, why and who with?

As for her mother's part in her upbringing, Mary learned that such was no more or less than could be expected from any other mother of the time. She being a wife, Mrs Nuttall naturally did what her husband expected of her. Her role as mother, and the times they lived in, dictated that she raised Doris the way that her husband, Reginald wanted the child to be brought up; his way and no other!

33 Silk Street was a large, six-bedroomed Victorian house and had been the family home of the Nuttall family since the reign of Queen Victoria. This large house had been passed down through inheritance from generation to generation. Doris had never lived elsewhere. The house was much grander in size than the parents of Doris ever required for their own personal use, and would have been way beyond the monetary reach of her father's purse, had he ever needed to purchase the property. While he lived though, Reginald Nuttall would never have considered selling his family home. To do so, would have been tantamount to admitting that he had been born into a lower social station than that of his father or his grandfather had enjoyed!

~~~

The tragic death of both parents occurred when Doris was aged twenty-one. One morning while crossing the road arm-in-arm, a passing lorry hit a cart, careered out of control, and struck them both down; killing them outright!

Overnight, Doris found herself rudderless with no one around to advise, instruct and order her life. She had become a relatively well-to-do woman who was no longer financially dependent on another. She inherited the large house, two thousand, and three hundred pounds, government bonds, a few hundred stocks and shares in Lloyds of London and her mother's assortment of jewellery.

Having become financially independent at such an early age provided Doris with the freedom to do whatever she wanted to do with her future. Such was a freedom rarely experienced by any young woman of the times.

Having acquired such liberty however, Doris found she was unable to handle this great responsibility alone. Her daily routine had always been in the control of her father since childhood and whatever his impact had been on her life, she found herself once more needing a man to depend upon and to help organise and manage her affairs!

~~~

The things that affected Doris more than anything she was to learn after her parents' death were revealed in the birth certificates of herself and parents, along with their birth and marriage certificates.

Foremost was the identity of her father. Doris discovered that the man she had called 'father' all her life, wasn't! When Doris first saw her birth certificate, in the space provided for her father's name to be inserted was written, 'Not known.' Her mother had conceived her out of wedlock.

Her parent's birth certificates also revealed that while the man she had always known as 'father' had been born in Liverpool, her mother had been born in County Clomel, Ireland. The marriage certificate of Mr and Mrs Nuttall, when viewed alongside Doris' birth certificate, revealed that her mother was four months pregnant on the day of her marriage to Reginald Nuttall!

The only pieces of information that Doris was never to learn was twofold; her own connection with Portlaw and the identity of her natural father.

Doris was never to learn that the precise location of her conception was beside the flowing river in the fields of Curraghmore in Portlaw, County Waterford, Ireland. Though Doris knew she had been 'delivered' in a private Maternity Hospital in Liverpool, she never learned that she had been 'conceived' in Ireland by a father who was Portlaw born and bred. His name was John Flaherty, a Monsignor who was the parish priest of Portlaw at the time!

Having been 'conceived' in Portlaw, was a fact that was to prove a lifesaver for Doris in years to come, especially as Roman Catholics are brought up believing that life begins at the point of conception, not the moment of earthly delivery!

~~~

Three months after the burial of her parents, the attentions of churchgoer Patrick Storey were highly welcomed by the grieving Doris, who viewed the situation more superficially than was perhaps wise.

Patrick was a man of Roman Catholic persuasion, who attended 'St. Anthony's Catholic Church' in Scotland Road as regularly as the parish priest served mass there.

The church was one of the oldest in Liverpool and had stood there since 1833. Doris' parents attended it, despite the distance from their family home. They had chosen it to become their regular church of worship because it was an imposing dwelling in the Liverpool skyline; a place they thought fit enough for a family of middle-class station and good breeding to be seen praying each Sunday.

Doris' parents were strict Catholics and ensured that their only daughter was also indoctrinated in the Catholic faith. Doris on the other hand, never really felt that she belonged to the Roman Catholic branch of religion any more than any other religious body. She knew that her own religious upbringing, or indeed that of any other, was largely a matter of chance. Had her parents been born Protestant or Jewish, Doris knew that she too would have been brought up Protestant or Jewish, and would probably have felt just as committed or non-committed to those religions as she was to Catholicism.

Nothing more than loneliness, familiarity, habit and weekend routine therefore ensured that Doris continued to attend Sunday service at 'St Anthony's' after the death of her parents.

Every week that Doris attended church following her parents' funeral, Patrick Storey would make a point of speaking with her after Mass and enquiring how she was coping. To tell the truth, Doris welcomed his attention. Indeed anyone's attention would have been gladly accepted, especially attention from such a sensitive and kind man as Patrick was.

Patrick was extremely patient in slowly courting and stealing the affection of Doris and without her fully knowing it at the time; he wanted her every bit as much as she required wanting. With the passing of each week, each word and every look that the couple shared convinced Patrick that the time was now ripe for the picking.

Patrick Storey eventually persuaded Doris to attend a brass band performance with him one sunny Sunday afternoon in the park where they would picnic. He used this occasion to kiss her, first tenderly and then more passionately when they were unsighted and free from the disapproval of public gaze.

Within a few months, Patrick had taken Doris out dancing twice and she had accompanied him three or four times to the cinema, as well as continuing with their Sunday outings to the park.

Patrick was forever the perfect gentleman in all his dealings with Doris. After their times out, he always insisted on escorting Doris back to her house and would stand in the street watching her until she entered and shut the house door.

Doris told Mary one evening that approximate nine months into their courtship, Patrick proposed to her. She said that at the time, though flattered to have received a proposal to marry, she remained surprised that it would occur so soon into their brief courtship period. She asked Patrick for a few days to consider his proposal, during which she concluded that it only seemed natural to accept his offer of marriage. She loved Patrick as a male companion and saw him as being a good man who would protect and respect her. He seemed to possess all the main attributes that go to make up a good husband.

"But in all honesty, Mary," Doris said, "I could not truthfully have said that I was 'in love' with him!" she added, "but it felt right at the time and it made me feel safe by marrying him."

They were married at 'St Anthony's' and the couple commenced married life living from the home of Doris.

Doris had given herself to Patrick; she had given her sacred promise to live with him 'til death do they part. She had sworn on oath to be a dutiful wife and she had given him the ownership of her property, as she was now by law, considered his. He in turn had given Doris his name to add to her own, making her a wife of the times, an appendage of his masculine identity.

~~~

It was difficult to sell a large house at the time of the nation's receding economy, so after getting married, Patrick suggested that they stay there until the economic climate improved before downsizing to a smaller and more manageable property.

Meanwhile, Patrick said that by partitioning three rooms off on the second floor and letting them out to single men of good standing, they might profit from their excess house space. Patrick and Doris agreed that they would rent out the additional rooms only as self-contained flats and not offer full board.

Since leaving school, Doris had never had the necessity of having to work outside the parental home. Being very bright, she had been encouraged by her father to take all the examinations she could, so that she might one day become a schoolteacher if she never married.

Doris was as clever as any male who was entitled to go to university, but the times governed that this was not an option open to her. Women could not matriculate or graduate from university, however clever they were, let alone become a member of one! The highly clever woman was permitted to attend lectures, sit examinations and even gain honours in those subjects. Being a woman however, they were unable to receive the degree to which, had they been men, their examinations would have entitled them.

'Why should these male bastions of privileged education be open to mere women who had no entitlement to vote' was the position men of the time generally adopted. As far as the vast majority of men was concerned, 'a woman's place was in the home, looking after the welfare of her husband and children, in that order!'

Having never had to work, Doris could see the sense in Patrick's proposition to make an extra £1000 unearned income annually from getting three tenants for one floor of their house.

The couple converted one floor of the house, where the three lodgers would have self-contained apartments. This tenant accommodation would include their own bedroom, lounge and small kitchen area, along with one large bathroom to share.

This enabled Doris and Patrick to earn an income from the property without having to put too much ongoing work into it, as well as keeping the spacious ground floor of the large house to themselves.

The tenants would see to themselves and only a weekly change of bedsheets and towelling would be required for Doris to provide in exchange for an income of twenty pounds every Friday night.

This arrangement suited Doris and Patrick nicely. They could earn additional income without feeling themselves servant to the working classes. Patrick did any handy work required throughout the house as well as being able to carry on with his daily work at one of the local factory's stock room. This left Doris to act out the role of homemaker and wife.

Doris had intended to ask Patrick for his consent for her to work in the capacity of part-time teacher until children arrived on the scene, but the one time she had raised the subject shortly following their marriage, Patrick told her directly, "No wife of mine will ever work outside the matrimonial home."

Though Doris would never have dared accused Patrick of being envious of the higher education she had received above his level of schooling, she sensed that he had always silently resented their educational differences.

Patrick had come from poorer family circumstances and had received no further schooling beyond the basic grounding. When she and Patrick first got together, Doris knew that Mr Nuttall would never have approved of such an unequal relationship had he been alive. Indeed, had he lived, he would have moved heaven and earth to prevent such a union occurring! The problem was that her husband Patrick also knew it to be a social mismatch, and inwardly felt he had married above his class.

As regarding their sexual compatibility in the bedroom, unfortunately there was none! Doris, like many wives of the time, saw it as being her duty to oblige the bedroom advances of her lawful husband, but never enjoyed the idea of being on demand to any man's sexual whim. When they did make love, she did not find the experience either satisfying or pleasurable and did her best to feign enjoyment so it would be over quicker.

Six months after their marriage, Patrick was 'called up' and sent to the battlefields of France. Doris found that looking after number 33 alone was a full time occupation and yet, she was inwardly pleased with keeping herself busy throughout the war.

When Mary and her two youngsters arrived on her doorstep, Doris found a friend with whom she could share female companionship, and the looking after of her daughters during the daytime providing her with more purpose in her life than she had previously experienced.

Upon hearing all this, Mary was pleased to learn that she her children were truly welcomed additions to the home of Doris instead of being mere inconveniences and hard work.

Chapter Thirteen: 'Sweet Surrender'

Mary found her job at the munitions factory hard yet endurable. The women there were always game for a laugh and would forever be larking about, trying to get each other into trouble with the male supervisors. There were three supervisors at the factory where Mary worked and all were male. The workforce was largely female, but the way that the supervisors spoke to them was often far from how one might expect any woman to be addressed by a man.

When the male workers left the factory to become soldiers, their wives became the new workforce in their absence. The foremen however, treated them no differently in approach or language. Little care was rarely taken in their use of foul language, which was often less refined than that of an army drill sergeant on parade with a bunch of new recruits.

Two of the three supervisors at Mary's place of work used coarse language as their prime means of enforcing compliance with the largely female work force, and the female staff were simply expected to take it without complaint or backchat. It was common practice for the factory women to hear some supervisor verbally abusing another female employer as though she was some prisoner of war.

"Get a fucking move on, woman! You're not in the bedroom now making up your face as though you've all day to spare. We're fighting a bloody war and unless you pull out the stops and learn to do your bit, you'll hand victory to the Huns. Now get a move on and stop that chattering. It's like listening to a fucking cattle market hearing you lot jabber. Get a move on!"

"I'll get a move on when that dozy git gets a hard on and starts waving it about over here so we can all do a bit of battering!" said Annie Bolton to her friend, Bessie Tahy.

"It's no good him waving it about in your direction, dear," Bessie replied laughingly, "you wouldn't know what to do with it if was staring you in the face!"

"It's not my face I'd be wanting it in!" replied Annie laughingly.

While Mary's ears had long heard the swear word 'faking' being spoken by man, woman and child alike back in Ireland and had accepted that word as being a natural part of Irish vocabulary, 'Fucking' seemed so crude and coarse a term in comparison. To hear it spoken both to women and by women was something that still had the power to offend her sensibilities.

Mary did her work in the munitions factory to the best of her abilities and mixed readily with the rest of the workforce. There were, however, a couple of women there who deeply resented Irish feet on English soil and would refuse to talk to her directly. If they needed to say something to Mary, they would speak to the woman who worked alongside her, as though Mary was invisible instead of standing there. "Ask your friend when she's going back home to where she belongs? Irish tinkers aren't welcome in these parts!"

Mary later learned that many Englanders refused to forget or forgive the Irish rebel for turning their guns against them during the Easter Uprising of 1916, when the British were already engaged in war, fighting in Europe against the Germans.

There was one young supervisor at the factory called Mark Stein who was obviously interested in Mary and would go out of his way with any excuse to talk to her whenever he could. Though nice enough in his own way, Mary was not interested in adding any further complications to her life right now, and to tell the truth, even had she been so inclined to either want or need a man, getting herself tied up with another work's supervisor could not have been farther from mind. There would be no more Sean Morrises in her life if she could help it!

~~~

Three months later, and after hearing no word from her husband Patrick since his first and only leave, Doris received an official telegram one Friday afternoon. The telegram informed her that her husband had been killed in action serving his country, along with two hundred and forty-three other men from his regiment in the height of battle.

Because of the heavy bombardment at the time of their deaths, not all the men could be positively identified; so the army had to be guided by the dog tags they later found upon the deceased soldiers and their scattered body parts. Doris learned that the dead soldiers were to be buried in a mass grave somewhere in the fields of Flanders, between the geographical regions of France and Belgium.

When Mary came home later that day, she discovered a tearful Doris staring with fixed eyes at a photograph of her husband Patrick that she clasped tightly in one hand. She had obviously spent most of the afternoon crying alone in her big house. Had it not been for her supervising the children, she told Mary that she did not know what she would have done.

Mary consoled Doris the best way she knew how, with a loving embrace and words of reassurance. Doris on the other hand, just cried intermittently and kept accusing herself for not having been a good enough wife to Patrick when he was alive.

"Now, now, Doris," Mary said," I'm sure there could have been no better wife he could have had."

"If only that were true, Mary, it would be some consolation in this sad hour, but alas, I'm afraid it isn't and I wasn't! I'm afraid that I wasn't then, and the cruelty of it all is that I wouldn't have met his expectations tomorrow either, had he returned safely to me from the war."

Later that night after Mary had put the children to bed and retired to her own bed, she was about to drop off to sleep when she heard a knock on her bedroom door and heard Doris quietly speak her name.

"Mary, it's Doris" the voice said from the other side of the door.

Mary opened the door and seeing her distressed friend standing there in her nightdress visibly shaking,

Doris said, "Can I…. can I come in with you tonight, Mary. I just can't sleep on my own tonight!"

"Of course you can," Mary said as she ushered her friend into her bed.

Mary got into bed and two minutes later, the couple were embracing each other to keep warm and comfortable. Throughout the night, the couple cuddled and Doris cried intermittently.

~~~

Mary awoke the following morning to find herself alone in bed. Doris had risen before her and had started to make breakfast for the two young sisters. With it being Saturday morning, though Mary had to work half a day until noon, she would be free until Monday morning after she had returned home mid-day.

Seeing her children's cots empty, Mary sensed that Doris had obviously had got them up, washed and dressed them and had taken them downstairs to her living quarters. By the time Mary had dressed and joined them downstairs, Doris had fed both children. The table was neatly set for two, ready for both women to eat.

Mary sat down and after the usual morning pleasantries, Doris joined her. Doris said, "I've cooked us both scrambled eggs and there's some warm toast and jam as well."

Mary coyly smiled at Doris and thanked her for her consideration.

"Think nothing of it, Mary," she replied. "You were there for me last night when I needed you and the least I can do is to be there for you this morning and make sure you get a well-earned lie in for an extra half hour before you get yourself off to work."

Nothing more was spoken between the two women that morning before Mary set off to work in the munitions factory, but both women knew that not all was quite as it should be between them. There were things that needed to be spoken of openly between them, subtle things that needed clarifying.

~ ~ ~

That morning at work, Mary was not her usual self. Something had happened during the past twenty-four hours, something between her and Doris, which indicated that nothing would ever be precisely the same again! All her thoughts that morning at work were not upon her job, but were instead on Doris and herself.

When Doris had asked to sleep in her bed last night, Mary had not given the matter a second thought under the circumstances. Indeed, it might have remained such had not the goodnight kiss that Doris given her before they both settled down to sleep been somewhat shorter and of less in intensity.

Then there was the way that Doris had caressed her as Mary fell off to sleep. That had been another sign of things to come, which Mary had naively missed. On one occasion during the night, Mary had awoken to find Doris's bare breast touching her own and their legs entwined in such a way that flesh touched flesh.

Mary looked at Doris laid beside her in bed. Her eyes were closed and her breathing held a calmness and regularity of pace that indicated she was peaceably asleep. Mary gently moved to uncouple her legs from

Doris without disturbing her bed companion and quietly turned her back.

As she lay there wide-awake, Mary started to imagine all manner of strange thoughts for the first time in her life, as well as coming to terms with the consequences of their nocturnal actions.

It was not their close proximity, not the touching of flesh upon flesh or the tightness of their embrace, which mildly disturbed Mary. It had not even been the hardening of her own breast nipples as they rested on Doris's breast. None of those things unsettled her thoughts and wild imaginings. What disturbed Mary was the fact she had found the overall experience unnaturally pleasurable!

All of her life Mary had dreamed of motherhood. All of her life she had prized this role at the heart of her needs. She had never viewed the intimate closeness with any man as having been highly sexually or overly pleasurable. To Mary, any such act had been a means to an end, something that was functionally necessary! For the first time in her life, Mary started to sense why this was so, and for the first time inwardly, she grew to know herself better! Last night with Doris had been more sensual an experience than she had ever felt, it had moved her more than having laid with any man!

Deep down, Mary knew she shared a love with Doris, a hidden love that had existed throughout the centuries between one woman and another, a love that dare not speak its name. A mere seven hours beside Doris in bed had stirred Mary in ways that no man's touch or her own wildest imagination had ever moved her. It was as if her life had clicked into place within the brief space of one day and night and for the first time ever outside of the role of motherhood, Mary could see purpose in another role; that of lover with another woman, that union between her and Doris!

~~~

Mary returned to number 33 after her shift that morning and found that Doris had dressed both children in preparation of taking them for a walk in the park that afternoon.

Little needed to be verbalised between both women regarding the previous night. It was not as necessary now since Mary had started to come to terms with her own feelings whereas Doris had already given the probability earlier consideration.

When the two women next looked at each other, their eyes spoke a conversation that was mutually and instantly understood; a conversation that had previously remained unsaid.

They all had a lovely afternoon in the park, during which each woman declared her love for the other. After the children had been put to bed for the night, Doris was the first to bring up the subject again.

"It now all makes sense to me, Mary, as to why that sexual spark was never there on my side with Patrick. I swear I had no inkling why at the time, though I gave the matter much thought once I accepted that it was not natural for a wife to feel as distant as I felt when we lay naked in bed and he wanted pleasuring. I swear, Mary, until last night, I was never quite sure why this was, though some suspicions lurked deep down."

"Now I know! Now that I know that I was never made to hold those sexual desires most women are supposed to have for a man, I feel a great weight lifted from me. Perhaps, through finding love with you, I will for the first time in my life, find not only true happiness, but also my real self. I love you, Mary Fanning. I love you and I always will. I thank God that you and your two girls knocked on my door and came into my life! I love you, lass!"

Being the less educated party of the two, whose own words would never have been able to capture the elegance and clarity of meaning as those spoken by Doris, Mary decided to say little in reply. She felt every bit as strongly as Doris did and she was every bit as passionate and as true in purpose. Mary decided that she would let her feelings speak for her instead.

She approached Doris and after telling her, 'I love you too, Doris' she kissed her on the lips, first tenderly and then more passionately.

"Faking hell ….. you're blowing my mind," Mary said as she pulled Doris closer to her. She wanted her close enough to share the same breath that lingered between their lips. This time there was no accidental touching of each other's breasts; each touch was deliberate. There was no uncertainty in the action between them, no need to exercise caution and no pulling away as passions started to ignite and arouse that insanity of touch, which drives one mad if not instantly satisfied.

"Not here" Doris said breathlessly. "Not here, Mary. Let us retire to your bed. We can be together there, as well as keep an eye on Nellie and Nora."

Five minutes later, both women were in bed together and each instantly knew, as they lay close in their nakedness that all was well with the world inside these four walls. Over the next hour, their warm bodies entwined in ecstasy and lifted them to the height of planes never before imagined possible!

As they drifted off to sleep in warm embrace, part of Doris felt extremely guilty that within a few days of hearing about the death of her husband Patrick, she was feeling the happiest she had ever felt in her life. Indeed, there was a poignancy in the unfolding of events, a sort of sweet bitterness and irony in the outcome.

Doris thought that the news of Patrick's death followed by her outpouring of tears and sadness at the time, had effectively proved her love diviner and the precipitator of her ultimate salvation; the very thing which had driven her into the arms of Mary.

Chapter Fourteen: 'The Early Years of the Two Sisters'

By the time that the two sisters, Nellie and Nora grew old enough to start attending school, their mother Mary and Doris had grown as close as any loving couple could. In fact, whenever needing to address either, the children called Mary, 'Mother' and Doris, 'Aunty Doris.' Thus, in the eyes of Nellie and Nora, they had always had two mother figures to care for them.

With regard to the love that dare not speak its name between Mary and Doris, unlike male homosexuals who would be imprisoned if discovered, there was no law prohibiting lesbianism, yet it was still regarded as a beastly act and highly repugnant.

It is thought that the reason such a law was never enacted was because the late Queen Victoria, when presented with the legislation that made homosexuality between both sexes illegal, insisted that 'ladies' did not do such things. It was her opinion that such things would be a physical impossibility between women. Consequently, the law forbidding lesbian activity was never legislated.

As far as wider society was concerned however, it held no such niceties of female morality and if two women were ever suspected of having too close a physical relationship, they would be gossiped about as being 'suspicious spinsters,' living in sin, being perverted and practising an inferior form of sexuality. If, however, proof of such an 'unnatural relationships' ever became common knowledge, the offending couple would be publically shamed and disowned as citizens of gross indecency, and considered unfit to live alongside decent folk! Upon discovery, they even had their heads forcibly shaved by the mob as a sign of the shame they carried.

In truth, there had always existed lesbians since God first made woman, and for hundreds of years, love and sex between two women had been downplayed and kept invisible from the public eye. As far as Mary and Doris were concerned however, it being new to them, they naturally intended to keep their personal relationship within the secrecy of their four walls. They did not intend to become the common gossip of malicious tongues.

~~~

Towards this end of 1921, Doris sold her Liverpool house. She, Mary and their two girls moved inland to Haworth in Keighley, West Yorkshire. Doris had downsized from a large Victorian house to a small two bedroomed Victorian terraced cottage in West Lane, Haworth. The house was close enough to village life without being stuck bang in the middle of the hustle and bustle of Main Street.

After the sale of Doris's larger property, the difference in house prices provided sufficient income with which to start up a little bakery business for Mary, supplying local shops from her home.

Mary had become the most proficient of bakers since arriving in England and made the best cake, buns and jam this side of the Irish Sea. Her speciality was 'Irish Teacake' and gooseberry jam, which turned out to be highly sought after by the locals.

In the privacy of her own home, whenever Mary would refer to her Irish Teacake she would call it 'Carol Law Cake', a practice that greatly amused Doris and the children. When they pressed her for her reason of giving the teacake this secret name, the answer Mary supplied could not have been simpler to understand.

Mary said, "A woman called Carol Law first introduced the cake to me as young woman shortly after my mother had died. I'd never tasted its like before. I loved it so much that when Carol Law died soon after, I 'borrowed' her recipe from the possessions she left behind, and after tweaking it, I made the Irish Teacake my own."

Doris had decided to return to the field of education shortly after arriving in Haworth and become a teacher in one of the local Primary Schools.

The most important reason for the family's move from Liverpool to West Yorkshire however, was the preservation of the relationship and secret love the two women held for each other. They decided that they would draw less attention to themselves in the future, if they were to start life anew as blood sisters living together; one a mother to two daughters, the other, their aunt, and both widows to the ravages of the 'First World War'.

The two women knew that rural communities, though often slow in accepting newcomers into their midst, invariably accepted what they were told upon first meeting, until or unless of course, they were to learn otherwise.

Having lived most of their lives with Mary and Doris since infancy made it an easy enough lie to convince the two children that their mum and 'Aunt Doris' were blood sisters and that the children's father and the late husband of 'Aunt Doris' had both died as serving soldiers in the war.

The two women did not feel bad about this deception to the children. They gauged that by the mere telling of an innocent lie, life for the family would proceed more smoothly and uncomfortable questions and neighbourly suspicions would be less likely to rear their ugly heads. They also withheld from the two sisters that each had been one of co-joined twins, whose twin had died before their birth. They believed that what they never knew about they could never miss.

~~~

As the children progressed in age through the various landmarks of their development, it became evident to both Mary and Doris that the two girls were not like any other two sisters they had ever heard of. In short, it was as though they shared every body part and experienced identical thoughts, feelings and actions of each other at precisely the same time!

Nelly and Nora Fanning were to live as closely in every way as two sisters had ever lived. They went everywhere together, did everything in unison and even spoke the same words at the same time; completing each other's sentences as though the words had been born within the same breath, despite having been voiced through two mouths simultaneously. They lived in the same house, shared the same room, slept in the same double bed and wore matching clothes.

The children attended the village Primary School and as the villagers grew to know them better over the months and years ahead, all believed the sisters to be so close that they experienced the same moment. It was as though they were in perfect communion with each other's existence.

There was only one life experience they did not share, apart from their Christian names. Each sister had a different guardian angel looking over her!

Every night since their birth, their guardian angels would stand at the foot of their cot/bed. Each guardian angel would appear as soon as their charge had gone to sleep and would disappear each morning a few seconds before the two sisters opened their eyes. Thus, the two sisters never knew their guardian angels stood vigil every night, yet they always sensed a presence of feeling constantly protected.

Whenever the two sisters asked questions about their birth, their mother would never tell them the full truth. She naturally wished to protect her daughters from unnecessary pain. She never told them about the premature death of their respective twins; the other half of them they would never know.

Mary had decided shortly after their birth that there was nothing to be gained by telling them that they had each been twins inside her womb, but that their respective twin had not survived the pregnancy! She did not wish them to have to grieve for a twin they never knew existed. She did not want them to feel the loss that she had felt; a loss, which would prevail throughout their lives, once informed that they were but two remaining of four.

~~~

When the two sisters attended first school in Haworth, their teachers found their behaviour strange while their classmates considered it frightening and somewhat sinister. The two sisters would sit beside each other at the front of the class and whenever the teacher asked one a question, both sisters would provide the same answer at precisely the same time! It mattered not whether the answer was accurate or inaccurate; the two sisters always voiced it together!

When one had cause to smile or grimace, the face of the other sister would bear the same look simultaneously, even when each were looking in opposite directions.

The first truly inexplicable incident, which told everyone in the school that the sisters were 'special', was when one of the bully pupils who disliked the positive attention which the teachers and classmates usually gave the sisters, decided to embarrass the duo.

The manner in which the bully chose to do this was to divide the two sisters and to reveal them to the rest of the class as being charlatans. The bully wanted Nellie and Nora Fanning to be seen as two separate beings who produced natural and individual responses when caught off guard, yet superficially contrived ones that mimicked 'twoness' at other times.

The bullyboy placed half a dozen marbles on the floor at the desk side of Nellie to make her slip and fall when she stood up. Not only did he intend to hurt one of the sisters, but he also wanted to humiliate both of them in the process. Therefore, he told the other pupils what he planned to do and threatened them with violence if they warned the two sisters.

At the end of the lesson, Nellie and Nora got up to leave the classroom. As Nellie stepped on the small glassy marbles, she stumbled and fell to the ground, screaming in pain as she broke a leg!

The bully laughed aloud seeing Nellie fall to the ground, but he and the rest of the class gasped to see Nora also fall at precisely the same moment from the other side of the desk where no marbles had been scattered. She too screamed in synchronised pain and broke her leg! When the bully looked more closely, he found that three of the six marbles he had placed at Nellie's desk side had rolled across the floor and had repositioned themselves at the side of Nora's desk!

Both girls returned home that day with their respective left legs in a plaster cast and with the medical instruction to take four weeks off school. They had broken their legs in precisely the same place!

This list of coincidences however, did not end there. Over the years ahead, the two sisters revealed themselves to have powers of such an unusual kind that to some, they seemed magical, while to others of more suspicious mind, they appeared unnatural and sinister!

The two sisters were to display their ability to foretell the future and be able to tune into the thoughts of another's mind. Without doubt, though, their most 'unnatural' gift ever displayed was their ability to heal by the simultaneous laying on of hands!

Their mother and Aunty Doris also learned of the special powers that Nellie and Nora possessed, and as they advanced through childhood from the years of five to fifteen, Mary and Doris knew they mothered children of exceptional quality and inexplicable ability.

As to the girls themselves, they never considered their ability to do certain things that others could not do as representing anything special. It was true that they believed themselves to be 'special,' but did not particularly consider any of the things they found natural to do as falling into the 'special' category.

A few incidents in their early lives will quickly illustrate such powers they possessed and will serve to show the nature of their instant effect and long-term impact they had on others.

When the two sisters spoke outside the presence of their mother and Doris, the spoke the same words simultaneously, but when they spoke in the presence of their mother and Doris only, they would each speak the alternate words of the same sentence. Their speech would usually involve Nellie beginning the sentence and Nora ending it. In between, Nellie would speak the first two words of the sentence and Nora the next two, Nellie the next two and Nora the next two, etc.

Having already experienced over nine years of this verbal behaviour from the two girls since they'd both spoken their first word in the same moment of life, mum and Doris now expected them to speak this way, and indeed, they would have found it strange had they not done so.

Their mother and Doris had already accepted that the two sisters were 'special', even long before the girls had displayed any of their other unusual behaviour and extraordinary abilities, which set them apart from their peers.

One night, both sisters awoke from a dream they had shared and the morning after, they told their mother and Doris what they had dreamt. At first, after hearing of their dream, neither woman could make head nor tail of its meaning.

In their shared dream, the two sisters had seen thousands of empty shops, deserted streets, abandoned buses and parked trains all over London. Everywhere in their dream they saw thousands of May Poles going around with ribbons hanging down and not one person attached to them or in sight.

"But what does it mean?" Doris asked. "Or does it not mean anything at all?"

"I don't know," Mary replied adding, "but if both sisters dreamt the same dream, whatever it signifies, whatever message it holds, my money tells me that it means much more than nothing at all!"

Within the following week, meaning was given to the dream of the sisters. Between May 4th and May 13th 1926, 'The General Strike' brought the country to a standstill. During this period, millions of workers laid down their tools, all public transport stopped running and the vast majority of shops closed down in sympathy with the miner's cause. 'The General Strike' was but part way through when Doris made the connection between it and the dream of the two sisters.

~~~

During their tenth year of life, after visiting a wishing well near their home in Haworth, both sisters had the strangest of experiences.

The well in question was almost three hundred years old and over the centuries; it had been the source of strange and mysterious tales. The story was that during the late 1620s, in the reign of Charles 1st, the witch trials that had plagued England for the previous fifty years suddenly ended.

According to Miriam Adamson, who was aged 109 and reported to be the oldest woman in Haworth and perhaps the whole country, the very last witch to die in England was Molly Mildew. Molly had lived in an old shack somewhere out on the Haworth Moor. Unlike the witches before her, who had been executed in their hundreds in England since the witch trials had begun, burning at the stake was considered as being too quick a death for Molly. So instead of being burnt by fire or drowned by water wheel dunking, a fishmonger who sometimes doubled as executioner, gutted Molly on a wooden slab while the cheering public watched the grizzly sight.

The executioner slowly slit open Molly's stomach so she would die painfully and after cutting out her inners, he wrapped the string of intestines around her neck as if to strangle her spirit and prevent her body ever knowing eternal rest.

After the execution and according to parish records, Molly's dismembered corpse was cast down 'Mildew's Well' at the side of Haworth Parish Church. The well was over one hundred and twenty feet deep.

Over the next two centuries, every woman who had a stillborn child, disposed of their babe's body down the well into a watery grave at its bottom. Some disposed children belonged to married women while other castaways were the offspring to unmarried ones. Tales told behind the bars of taverns also spoke of some unwanted babies being cast down the well by their mothers whilst still alive; especially in cases where the child showed signs of mental deficiency or on occasions when a son was wanted, but a daughter had been born instead!

For nigh on three centuries, 'Mildew's Well' kept the darkest secrets and most wicked acts ever committed in the Parish of Haworth. Initially, locals regarded the well as a haunted place, the roundest of tombs, where many swore they often heard the cry of a child come from deep inside. It was also rumoured that if one placed one's nose as far inside the well as was possible, the stench of death attacked one's nostrils and became overwhelming!

Over the passage of time, 'Mildew's Well', which had started life as the most sinister of places, underwent a transformation in the eyes of Haworth villagers. During the late 19th century, after the three

Bronte Sisters had placed Haworth on the map, making it a tourist place for literary pilgrims of the world to visit, the well gradually lost its old history and took on a new one.

In order to attract a greater number of visitors to the village, along with the increased custom they brought with them, all past and sinister history of the well was conveniently written out of village memory. Even the Parish records of the church that recorded births and deaths since the days of Oliver Cromwell mysteriously vanished from public eye. Instead of remaining a well of despair, doom and death, villagers started to promote 'Mildew's Well' as being a well of hope; a wishing well that brought good luck to all who looked into it and received its message with good heart!

Those older villagers, who had heard different tales in their youth about the well of death, were bribed to keep quiet by a publican promise of one free pint per week, along with providing a slate of their custom.

It was rumoured that if a person looked down the well and remained looking down it for a full ten seconds, they would hear a voice from one of their ancestors.

~~~

At ten years of age, the two sisters followed the village ritual of looking down the wishing well, one positioned at each side of the well. When they next lifted their heads, their faces shone brightly, very much as the faces of angels are supposed to shine. Each sister had heard a voice from the well. It was a voice from their past conveying an important message. The voice each sister heard was a different voice!

The voice provided both sisters with identical tasks to carry out before sleeping that day and the voice instructed each sister not to tell any other; including their sister. While finding this instruction to exclude their sister, with whom all secrets before had always been shared, strange indeed, both Nellie and Nora did precisely as their voice from the well had commanded them.

The voice instructed them to write each other a letter and to leave the letter sealed and unopened until the dawn of their fortieth birthday. Both sisters carried out the instructions as specified by their voice of the wishing well and kept their sealed letters safely bound.

When the sisters were aged twelve, a horse-drawn runaway cart ran over a black cat in Main Street, in the centre of Haworth Village. The poor creature's cries of pain were pitiful to the ears of all onlookers as the runaway horse and cart crushed the cat beneath its metal-rimmed cartwheels. The two sisters heard the whelps of the crushed creature and approached it. The cat had been crushed so badly that its head was now misshapen. The two sisters each laid a hand of compassion on the bleeding cat as it slumped close to death, its breathing on the brink of extinction.

One minute later, the cat moved. It had miraculously survived its near death experience. It suddenly jumped up and sprightly ran away from the scene of the accident, up the nearby steps at the side of

'The Bull' tavern, towards the church graveyard off Main Street.

The villagers of Haworth who named it 'Lucky', later adopted the black cat and would feed it daily. The cat itself became a landmark as it increased in size with all the village treats it received. Lucky lived in the church graveyard until the end of its days. Ever since that day, a black cat (presumably a descendant of Lucky), has lived in the Parish Church graveyard and each black cat has grown exceedingly fat on the amount of daily tit bits!

As Mary saw all this, her mind went back to the runaway horse and cart that had collided with her own father many years ago, and which had rendered him a virtual cripple. She silently thought at the time of seeing the miraculous resurrection of the cat, 'If only I'd had the benefit of my daughters' healing hands then!"

Chapter Fifteen: 'Doris becomes unwell'

Life proceeded very satisfactorily with the family during their years in the village of Haworth. Doris soon settled into the school where she worked and within six months, Mary, who was to become the best of cake makers for miles around, constantly baked in the kitchen of her home, fulfilling the regular orders from five shops in the village and two shops in the nearby village of Oakworth.

The two sisters, Nellie and Nora, would rarely attend village events outside the company of their mother and Doris. Having now reached the age of sixteen, they had started to look more grown up and more attractive.

While the boys at their school could see the attractive womanly features that the two sisters possessed, none was brave enough to ask either sister out on a date. Their peers viewed their behaviour as 'strange' at best bordering on 'sinister' and no boy in the school dared risk the perceived dangers of being alone with either sister. They seemed forever fearful that they might cast a spell on them, were they ever to displease.

The two sisters however, did not have the slightest inclination or desire to enter the dating scene that all the other girls seem to seek and constantly talk of. Nellie and Nora could not understand what it was that made the company of bossy boys so desirable a thing to preoccupy the mind of any girl!

Instead of going around with their schoolmates, the two sisters preferred to keep to themselves; with the only other welcomed company being that of their mother and Aunty Doris.

The sisters would spend their leisure hours helping their mother with her homemade cake business. There would always be work to do in this respect, helping with the baking preparations, cleaning and washing up and delivering the finished product to all the customers in Haworth and nearby Oakworth.

As the two sisters approached their 18th birthday, their mother asked them if they would prefer their own space by occupying their own bedroom or at least having their own bed to sleep in.

When Mary asked this question of them, both daughters looked back at her as if the question had been too asinine to pose. It was obvious by their looks of disdain that Nellie and Nora had no desire to be separated at the age of eighteen years any more than they had during previous years.

Nellie and Nora, although clever at school, did not want to advance their education after they had taken their school examinations. University life was not for either of them. Neither had they any desire to obtain an ordinary job outside the family home where they would simply become the subjects of prurient observation. After some discussion, their mother consented to let them work at home alongside her in her cake-making venture.

~~~

One Monday evening, Doris arrived home breathless from the school where she taught. She slumped down in the chair as soon as she came in and looked very pale. Mary dropped what she was doing at the time and made Doris a nice warm cup of tea with two spoons of sugar.

"Get that down you, Dory," she said. Dory was Mary's newest pet name for her partner, which she called her when the two of them were alone.

Doris drank the tea and then retired to bed early, thinking that she was perhaps coming down with some infection she had caught at school. When Mary went to bed around 11pm after she had prepared some work for tomorrow, she found Doris fast asleep so left her undisturbed. As Doris slept, Mary heard her heavy and irregular breathing.

The following morning, Doris asked Mary to call down to the school for her as soon as the head arrived and tell her she would be having a few days off work due to some mild illness she was experiencing. Mary asked the girls to keep an eye on Doris while she visited the school with the message.

Later, when Mary returned from her school errand, she called upstairs to check on Doris. Doris was still looking very poorly so Mary insisted upon sending out the girls to request that the doctor make a home visit later this morning.

Doctor Brown visited their home around 11.30am, after he had cleared his morning surgery at the Health Centre. He examined Doris while Mary waited down stairs, making a pot of tea. When the doctor had finished his examination, he came downstairs. His face carried a look of concern upon it.

"What is it?" Mary asked Doctor Brown, "What is it Doctor?"

"I'm afraid it's bad news," the doctor replied. "It looks like your sister could have a lung disease, but we won't know for sure until we get some x-rays done at 'Bradford Royal Infirmary'.

"What can we do for her meanwhile?" Mary asked Doctor Brown.

"She must rest completely and let's hope it does not worsen," the doctor replied. "I'll arrange to get her x-rayed as soon as possible to confirm the diagnosis."

During the following week, Doris was x-rayed at the hospital. Unfortunately, the feared diagnosis was confirmed. Doris had cancer of the lung and it was in its later stage. The x-rays revealed large shadows showing that both lungs were cancerous.

Mary seemed to take the news far worse than her partner did, despite it being Doris who faced the inevitable death sentence.

~~~

Over the following week, Doris's condition worsened and the doctor visited her home daily. Doris was offered hospital admission, but as her condition had passed the stage where it was operable, Doris decided that were she to die, she would choose to die at home with Mary and the girls and not on a sick hospital ward or in some isolated side room.

Once it became clear that Doris was not going to improve in her health, even temporarily, Mary told both sisters the probable outcome and warned them to prepare for the worse over the weeks ahead.

Mary and Doris cried a great deal together during the immediate weeks after learning of the confirmed medical findings. Then, when things looked to be at their worse, something very strange happened, which was to lead both women to know that the girls they looked after was indeed truly 'special'.

After the two sisters had learned of the stated condition of their Aunt Doris, they refused to accept the doctor's prognosis that she would shortly die. Something deep inside told the two sisters that they could help Doris. When Doris was at her worse, the two sisters decided it was time to intervene.

Their mother knew that there was nothing to lose by going along with her daughters. She believed if anyone could help Doris, they could.

For four days and nights, the two sisters sat by the side of their Aunt Doris' bed. They refused to leave her room and insisted that they ate and slept at the side of her bed until she pulled through. Throughout their vigil, the healing hand of both sisters remained placed upon the lungs of the dying woman.

For four nights and days, the two sisters carried out this hands-on healing ritual and on the morning of day five, Doris miraculously started to get better. Mary was over the moon and could hardly believe her eyes to see the daily improvement in her partner. Doctor Brown was simply flabbergasted when it became apparent that his patient was getting better instead of worse!

Thinking his stethoscope to be faulty and in need of urgent replacement after he'd listened to the patient's lungs, the doctor arranged to have Doris x-rayed at the hospital again. When the results came back, he started to question all the medical training he had acquired since leaving university.

The x-rays no longer revealed the presence of the patches on her lungs, which had previously shown up. Doctor Brown felt there must have been some mistake, some administrative mix up, and so he insisted that Doris be x-rayed again. Once more, the x-rays came back, revealing her lungs were clear of all manner of infection!

That was the moment when both women knew that the two sisters possessed inexplicable powers; powers of a supernatural kind. Never again, would either woman question the sisters as to the source of their powers; in future, they merely accepted their presence.

The sisters did try their laying on of hands again with other creatures close to death, but apart from Lucky the black cat and Aunty Doris whom they brought back from the brink of death, there were no other miracles.

~~~

Throughout the Second World War years 1939 to 1946, Doris continued to work as a schoolteacher and during the last six months of the war years, Mary returned to work in the Royal Ordinance Factory at

Steeton, approximately eight miles from Haworth, and put her home business on hold until the war had ended.

Mary and Doris had a happy existence together and throughout their lives, no villager ever suspected the two women to hold any closer relationship than one of sisterhood. As to the two sisters, Nellie and Nora, they were to continue living within the same house as their mother and Aunt Doris until the older women died.

~~~

Two months before the end of 1956, the two sisters celebrated their fortieth birthdays and exchanged the letters they had written to each other at the age of ten years as instructed by the voice from the well.

Each letter told the other sister the secret they had learned after their visit to the well as children. The two sisters learned that they had each been co-joined twins throughout their mother's pregnancy, but had been born without their co-joined twin, who had died in their mother's womb. Nellie learned that her twin sister had been given the name of Nancy and Nora learned that her twin sister had been called, Maureen.

Each sister was told that until their deaths, their deceased twin would be their Guardian Angel and would stand at the foot of their bed nightly to protect and watch over them until they awoke the following day.

Nellie and Nora felt blessed to have their own Guardian Angel look over them and each felt more complete to know their names of Nancy and Maureen.

~~~

Two months after their fortieth birthdays, the family house in Haworth was partly destroyed in the middle of the night when all four occupiers were fast asleep in their beds. It was around 3am in the early morning when the explosion occurred at the cobblers, next door. A gas leak had developed and when the owner went to investigate the smell and turned on the light downstairs, the leaking gas main exploded.

The dwelling next door was completely demolished along with half of the upstairs in the neighbouring home of Mary, Doris, Nellie and Nora. Both adults and a child who occupied the cobbler's dwelling were killed outright, along with Mary and Doris who slept in their beds on this side of the partitioned wall that adjoined both properties. The explosion did not touch the other side of the house where Nellie and Nora now slept.

The two sisters were deeply shocked by the tragic deaths of their mother and aunt and despite whatever mysterious powers they possessed; neither had experienced any premonition about the tragic explosion that was to divide their family in two on that fatal night.

For a full three months after their deaths, their need to grieve was great. This was the only time in their lives when the two sisters were known to cry.

Nellie and Nora found the funerals of their mother and Aunt Doris almost too much to bear. Their mother and aunt were buried in Haworth Parish Church of 'St Michael and All Angels' whose one-time curate, the Reverend Patrick Bronte, had ministered there from 1819 onwards. Patrick Bronte had been the father of the three famous, literary sisters of Haworth, the authors, Charlotte, Emily and Anne.

After the burial of their mother and Aunt Doris, the two sisters had no desire to continue living in Haworth. They felt that destiny decreed that the time for them to move on had arrived and that a new phase of life awaited them in another place. For them, Haworth had lost all pleasure and purpose and to remain there without their mother and Aunt Doris, would not have been the same.

~~~

Following the family home having been properly rebuilt, the sisters sold the property and moved back to the land of their birth to live out the remainder of their days. Naturally, there was only one part of Ireland to which they were drawn; Portlaw, County Waterford.

The two sisters had attained a certain notoriety during their years living in Haworth, a notoriety that was to find its way back to County Tipperary long before their return. You see, Nellie and Nora were not the only two residents of Haworth Village who had been born in Ireland.

There were another two Irish villagers called Claire Downy and Brigit Doggery. Claire and Brigit had left their homes in County Tipperary twenty years earlier. They had each married local Yorkshire chaps and set up home in Haworth. Naturally, never a week went by without either of them dropping a line to their family in Tipperary, the neighbouring county to Waterford.

When Irish women chat together, they tend to chat for hours on end. Separate them by three hundred miles of Irish Sea and make their only communication one of letters, they become no different. They remain muck spreaders, character destroyers, gossip transmitters and the conveyor of mystery and miracles!

When Claire and Brigit wrote home to their parents weekly, they rarely wrote less than a dozen pages of gossip each. It was only natural for them to mention in their letters, the two mysterious sisters from the Emerald Isle with the power to speak in one breath, prophesise future events, read thoughts and bring dead cats back to life by their laying on of hands!

For a number of years now, news of the mysterious powers of the two sisters had found its way back to the families of Claire Downy and Brigit Doggery in County Tipperary, a mere distance of ten miles from Portlaw in County Waterford.

Long before Nellie and Nora Fanning next set foot back on Irish ground, their reputation as fortune-tellers, mind readers, and wielders of mystical powers had preceded them! The people of Portlaw knew not whether they be welcoming back into their midst, witches or miracle workers.

It was rumoured by some Portlaw residents that the two sisters would join a convent or even establish a religious Order of their own, where they might live out the rest of their lives. A few of the less charitable and more suspicious villagers said they would be more likely to hold a witches' coven up Curraghmore on every full moon!

Chapter Sixteen: 'Back where it all began'

During their fortieth year of life, Nellie and Nora returned to live in Portlaw. Initially, they tried to buy the home where their mother had once lived at, 14, William Street, but the present owner initially declined their offer for it, stating adamantly that he had no inclination to sell his home at any price.

Within one week however, word about the two sisters had spread around Portlaw and all the villagers were speaking about the mysterious events, which had surrounded them in Haworth, West Yorkshire. Gossip was rife about their strange behaviour and the sinister powers they were said to possess.

When the reluctant seller learned of the two sisters' ability to see into the future, as well as possessing the power to heal by their 'laying on of hands', he began to fear for his person. He was afraid that if he held out against the offer of the two sisters to buy his house, they might put a witch's curse on him and turn him into a frog, or much worse, an Englishman!

This fear led the owner of 14, William Street to have second thoughts about the generous offer he had initially turned down from Nellie and Nora. He therefore changed his mind and decided to sell up to the two sisters and move house to another county.

Within one month of them having set foot back in the Village of Portlaw, Nellie and Nora became the proud owners of 14, William Street. Portlaw was the place where they had started in life and it was only fitting that they ended their days there.

~~~

Over the years ahead, most Portlaw villagers gradually accepted the two sisters in their midst as being a force for good. They came to see Nellie and Nora as two women who had been born 'special people', two sisters blessed by the hand of God and protected by angels on high.

The two sisters quickly came to command the respect of most villagers and even their strange behaviour of speaking simultaneously to outsiders was accepted. Initially, that which they first saw as being unnatural in their mannerism, the villagers of Portlaw eventually accepted as being spiritual.

Within the remaining fifty-nine years of their life, the fear that the two sisters first generated gradually turned to feelings of respect, before settling somewhere between feelings of admiration, love, adoration and finally, feelings of perceived saintliness!

~~~

The people of Portlaw frequently went to the two sisters with their problems, illnesses or in search of their wise advice. Once the sisters had provided counsel, the villagers treated their words as being no less than sacred.

The two sisters slept in the same bed until the end of their days and throughout their sleep, they would mirror the nightly behaviour of each other. They fell asleep and awoke the very same moment as each other. When one snored gently, so did the other. When each dreamt, they shared the same dream. Every thought by them was born from single mind, every thought united in single, steadfast purpose.

Nellie and Nora continued to have regular dreams about future events and before their third year back home in Portlaw, many of the villagers preferred to have the two sisters lay their healing hands upon their ill instead of making the village doctor their first point of call.

Though the two sisters often displayed their ability to prophesise future events, they were nevertheless unable to change the inevitable outcome of what they saw. Such advanced knowledge of pending doom weighed heavy on them, particularly in those situations, which resulted in the loss of life and limb. Their hurt was at its highest when they foresaw the death of innocent children.

The two sisters prophesised 'The Troubles' as they became known. 'The Troubles' were a conflict between Catholic and Protestant in Northern Ireland, which spilled over at times into parts of the Republic of Ireland and the mainland of England. The sisters even foretold of the year that the conflict would end in 1998 in Belfast with the signing of 'The Good Friday Agreement'.

For over half a century, Nellie and Nora suffered the advanced pain of bereavement for their fellow Irish men, women and children because of them dreaming about future events and tragic consequences.

The aspect which grieved the sisters the most about their bad dreams however, was the fact that despite knowing precisely what would happen in the future, to whom, when, where and why, there was not a thing they could do to stop the incident or influence the outcome!

In 1962, the two sisters shared a dream of a future event to be welcomed. They informed the villagers of Portlaw that the President of the United States of America, John F. Kennedy, would be visiting the Republic of Ireland on June 26th, 1963, one year hence. They indicated that he would fly into Dublin on the stated date. The two sisters dreamt this dream six months before the Whitehouse staff and the President had even planned it!

The foretelling of this momentous event enabled the people of Portlaw who acted upon it, to make advance arrangements for a Dublin visit the following year before all the city accommodation had been booked up by foreign tourists. Many of them were to pay for their trip to Dublin and stay there, from the winnings they would make at the bookies, having placed an advanced bet that the President of America would indeed visit Ireland before the end of June 1963!

Because of the 'tip off' the villagers of Portlaw had received from the two sisters, numerous large bets by most men and women from Portlaw were placed with the Waterford Turf accountants. Being so far in advance, they received very long betting odds between 500 and 1000-1. After the massive pay out, every bookmaker within a twenty-mile radius from Waterford became bankrupt!

Once the bookies learned of the powers of the two Portlaw sisters to foretell the future, no bookmaker between County Cork in the south and County Sligo in the north ever again took another bet from any Portlaw man, woman or child while the two sisters still drew breath!

By far the very worst dream that the two sisters ever had was during their 82nd year of life. This dream foretold of the wicked car bombing in Omagh, County Tyrone on the 15th August 1998.

The Real Irish Republican Army, a Provisional Irish Republican Army splinter group who opposed the I.R.A.'s ceasefire and the Good Friday Agreement, had perpetrated the bombing.

The bombing ultimately killed 31 people (including a mother pregnant with twins) and injured some 220 others. This carnage and loss of life was the highest death toll from a single incident during 'The Troubles'.

This dream haunted the two sisters for many months before the indiscriminate bombing occurred on the main street of Omagh and every year after on the anniversary of the deadly explosion. They had learned over many years, of the futility of attempting to warn anyone of the carnage that was to come. All they could do was to wait in cruel anticipation and publicly mourn in silent advance.

None of the people from Portlaw ever knew anything of the two sisters' darkest dreams that forewarned death and doom. Whenever the sisters had a dream relating to the death of another/others, they kept the knowledge to themselves. Only the most discerning of villagers initially suspected that some tragedy was imminent when they saw the two sisters out and about the village dressed in mourning black with a veil across their face.

In time, the mourning clothes of the two sisters would indicate to all villagers that death loomed large for some poor soul outside the boundary of Portlaw and that the two sisters were grieving out of respect for the loss to come!

~~~

One strange aspect about the two sisters' powers was the distinction between 'who', 'when' and 'where' they became operative and 'with what effect'. These four aspects of consideration determined in some measure the accurate foretelling of future events and the successful laying on of hands, which led to the curing of illness and the saving of life.

With regard to the limitations of their prophesy, while the two sisters could foresee future events about any country in which they happen to live, the range of their powers did not extend to seeing future events about any place outside the country of their residence. Neither did their powers to see such future happenings allow them to alter the foreseen outcome.

In addition, their capacity to heal and save life was only possible on a person/creature who had been Portlaw born and bred or who resided there. It was not until their later years of life that they realised that the black cat they brought back to life in Haworth, West Yorkshire must have been born from a litter of kittens in the village of Portlaw, Ireland, along with any other person whose life they had saved, such as their Aunt Doris!

The two sisters came to understand that their healing performed on any Portlaw villager or person born in Portlaw, would be effective wherever the subject was presented to them, whatever the nature of their illness or extent of their condition!

The only exception when the two sisters did not have the power to save the life of a Portlaw resident was when the injury or death of that person had been deliberately plotted and carried out by another Portlaw resident with sinister or murderous intent.

~~~

During the years ahead, the powers of the two sisters were to have an enormous effect upon the people of Portlaw. Over time, the doctor in Portlaw gradually became redundant, along with Harry Forde, the part time undertaker in the village.

You see, for a period of fifty-nine years until the two sisters died, no other Portlaw resident went to their graves. The only Portlaw residents to die during these six decades were the ones secretly poisoned or murdered by their unhappy spouses or cheated lovers.

With the remainder of the parish enjoying remarkably good health and the almost extinction of Portlaw deaths, there was insufficient business for either doctor or funeral director to ply their trade.

Over the next half century, Portlaw held the record for the world's oldest man, the world's oldest woman and the world's oldest married couple, as well as being able to boast of having the only living great, great,

great, grandfather ever known! In addition, over half of the entire population of Portlaw was aged in excess of 100 years and the General Post Office required an armoured truck to carry the weekly pensions!

~~~

Nellie and Nora Fanning never missed a Sunday morning attending the Catholic Church in Portlaw and the front pew was always left vacant for them to sit there as honoured citizens of the village.

As the years passed by, their fame spread everywhere across Ireland. Indeed, many a person from hundreds of miles away would travel to Portlaw in pilgrimage to see the two sisters. Many would bring their sick relatives in the hope they might receive the healing touch. Some came with empty water containers, which they would seek filling from the tap in the home of the two sisters, believing such water to be blessed with magic properties.

Some pilgrims would be crippled with arthritis, others, wheelchair bound or suffering from some other malady which plagued their lives. Often, half a dozen with an incurable terminal illness would come to see the two sisters of Portlaw, in the hope of receiving a miracle cure. All would plead for the two sisters to 'lay hands on them' and most became angry and aggrieved and felt bitterly cheated when a miracle was not performed.

The two sisters were content to lay hands on the site of the pilgrim's body afflictions, but never promised healing as a likely outcome. Some seemed content to receive the touch of the two sisters while most resented the apparent discrimination of their healing powers, which seemed to be confined solely to the residents of Portlaw.

Eventually, the two sisters were requested by the 'Portlaw Town Council' to stop performing their 'laying on of hands' upon the thousands of visitors who arrived in the village daily. Village life had become intolerable ever since word of the sisters' powers had spread to the four corners of the land. On every single day of the week now, over fifty busloads of visitors would descend upon Portlaw like a swarm of locusts seeking out the two sisters, the house where they lived and the church that they attended.

The shops, pubs and even the Catholic Church of Portlaw was initially highly pleased to have the increased business of the visitors and the additional revenue they brought, but once the village had become too crowded, a land mass night and day, every day of the year, all peace in the Parish of Portlaw quickly came to an abrupt end.

Before long, all the things that went to make up the character of the village and which the residents had grown to love began to disappear. Portlaw was no longer the lovely place it used to be!

The straw that broke the camel's back was the when busloads of Protestants from Belfast started coming down from the North of Ireland to visit Portlaw every day of the week throughout the entire year. That was when the 'Portlaw Town Council' decided enough was enough and that the time had arrived to call a halt.

From opening to closing hours daily, every pub in Portlaw had every inch of floor space filled with visitors from all four corners of the land. With pubs crowded, it was impossible to see the bar, let alone get close enough to order a pint!

Even, many of the Protestants from the troubled north who had heard of the numerous miracles performed by Nellie and Nora Fanning, wanted to see the two sisters for themselves before converting to Catholicism!

The Town Council and even the Parish Priest saw this sudden change as being one-step too far! Were large numbers of Belfast Protestants to decide to convert to Catholicism overnight, the Ulster loyalist's militant groups from Belfast would be outraged in new rebellion! It was feared that they would probably respond by sending daily bombing parties into the village of Portlaw, blowing up the Catholic Church during Sunday Mass when it was packed to the rafters and shooting everyone on sight!

By and large, Portlaw had kept itself and its citizens relatively free from 'The Troubles' since they had started. The overwhelming majority of the bombing and shootings between the warring factions in Ireland tended to be confined to the six northern counties of partition, and in particular, Belfast and Derry.

The villagers of Portlaw, particularly the town drinkers, preferred to drink their Guinness quietly, propping up the bar and talking about war with the Protestants without ever needing to engage in it!

It was the lively tune of fiddler and accordion player they wished to hear in the background of their conversations and quiet drinking, not the cries of innocent bystanders being blown to bits by planted bombs before they had emptied their beer glass!

Indeed, the only troubles that Portlaw had known since the British Army had been deployed in Northern Ireland in August 1969, was of minor proportion.

While the folks of Derry and Belfast were blowing each other to bits, what Portlaw had experienced during 'The Troubles' was small beer by comparison.

Portlaw 'troubles' were largely home-grown and included the temporary interference in the village's electricity supply during a bad storm of 1971 along with the rationing of two glasses of Guinness to each pub patron during a three-day strike of the Guinness factory workers in 1976.

There was also a fistfight between John Grogan and Doc Morrissey in 1977. This was over the affair that had taken place between Doc Morrissey and John's wife, Molly Grogan. When her husband had been laid up in hospital for three weeks, Molly Grogan was laid up with Doc Morrissey in Jim Ruffin's barn as they rolled around in the hay!

The fight lasted forty minutes and went on so long that both men retired to the pub for half a glass of Guinness half way through it, before resuming their battle in the street outside. The fight eventually spread from pub into the Village Square before the Parish Priest, Father McGuire stopped it and later read out the names of both men during the following Sunday Mass to shame them.

Then in June 1978, there was the falling out between the Portlaw families of Walker and Butt. The neighbours Jenny Walker and Sean Butt of William Street were the main protagonists in the slaying and the vendetta that followed.

Jenny Walker accused the youngest Butt son of stealing the Walker's piglet that lived on a piece of waste ground behind the Walker house.

The Walker family went to bed on the night in question and awoke next day to find an empty pigsty. During the night, Jenny Walker had been aroused from her sleep by a squealing pig and immediately went to her bedroom window and looked out. In the distance, she thought she saw the silhouette of neighbour Sean Butt walking away from the area of the waste ground with a squealing pig wriggling beneath his arm.

Jenny Walker had a reputation in Portlaw for being a heavy drinker. She was known as a woman, who drank far too much stout, far too often for her own sense of wellbeing. Subsequently, most folk refused to hold her account of the disappearing pig as being wholly credible.

On the night before the pig went missing, Jenny Walker went to sleep, as drunk as a skunk and could not in all honesty know whether she had really seen what she said she had seen through her bedroom curtains, or whether she had been dreaming!

For months later, all the Butt children were daily seen walking around the village eating bacon butties and grinning as wide as Kilkenny Cats as they threw the rind of their rashers into the Walker garden.

Though it was never proved beyond a shadow of doubt as to who the pig thief had been, Jenny Walker knew deep down that Sean Butt was the one responsible for stealing their pig and then getting the rest of his large family to eat the evidence.

Chapter Seventeen: 'The Portlaw Legacy'

When the sisters were in their 88th year, they both fell and incurred identical spinal injuries, which greatly affected their mobility thereafter and necessitated their use of walking sticks to get around.

Over the coming years, Portlaw residents fell into a silent conspiracy and kept the power of the two sisters for their eyes and ears only. As long as Portlaw villagers continued to benefit from their presence and touch, few cared too greatly, what occurred beyond the parish boundary! Besides, no villager wanted to start another stampede of miracle chasers swarming their quiet country village.

~~~

When the sisters were 99 years old, both had foreseen the ending of their life revealed through a shared dream. Indeed, their Guardian Angels told them as they slept, where, when and how their lives on earth would end.

They were informed by their Guardian Angels that the date of their departure from this life would be Thursday, May 14th, 2015, 'The Feast of the Ascension'. The place of their death was identified as the Holy Mountain of Croagh Patrick, which overlooks Clew Bay in County Mayo.

Before the day in question, the two sisters had made their way out to Croagh Patrick and had stayed overnight in one of the farmhouses there that catered for guests. This enabled them to get to the base of the mountain for their climb at dawn, next day.

The morning of their climb had started misty and the weather forecast signalled much denser mist to descend around noon.

The two sisters, aided by their walking sticks, started to climb the holy mountain. Each sister walked slowly, holding a walking stick in their left hand and a set of rosary beads in their right, with which they prayed throughout their journey.

Two local farmers saw the sisters start their climb and after seeing their twisted and aged bones and the snail's pace of their walk, they could not believe their eyes, particularly when they saw the two old women throw down their walking sticks towards the ground. Concerned for the safety of the two sisters, the farmers phoned the Garda.

There was a climbing ban on the Mountain that day, which ensured that the two sisters would be the only trespassers.

As the two sisters made their slow climb up the Reek, (a derivative from the word 'rick' or 'stack'), they each received an instruction from their Guardian Angel to cast their walking sticks to the ground. This they did and then continued to walk the stony path ahead.

Upon touching the ground, both walking sticks instantly transformed into snakes. A few seconds later, the two snakes crawled in front of the two sisters up the mountain. It was as though their Guardian Angels had smoothed their passage up the mountain by guiding them through the ever-thickening mist.

Soon it became no longer possible for the human eye to see any farther than mere inches ahead as the mist became denser than it had ever appeared in the past two hundred years. By now, the two sisters could no longer see the crawling snakes, so they followed the path of the rattlers by the sound of their hiss.

As the sisters slowly climbed, they thought about the holy ground upon which they walked and realised it would be their last walk upon this earth.

Croagh Patrick has reputedly been a site of pagan pilgrimage since 3,000 B.C., but became a site of Christian Pilgrimage after Saint Patrick had fasted on its summit for forty days and forty nights in the fifth century A.D.

Both sisters soon dropped out of sight of the watching farmers below and as the mist thickened, they even lost sight of each other. It was as though a cloak of thick fog had engulfed them and swallowed them up. They were never seen again!

For the next fourteen hours, dense mist concealed the Holy Mountain. Throughout the night, residents who lived in the farm dwellings and cottages below at the mountain base heard a constant hissing of snakes. The snake noises were so loud that one thousand rattlers could not have produced such sound.

After the mist had cleared the very next day, a search party climbed the mountain looking for the two old sisters, but they were nowhere to be found; not even their walking sticks, which the two watching farmers had seen them cast to the ground in the distance.

All manner of story began to spread about the mysterious disappearance of the two sisters on Croagh Patrick in the immediate years that followed. Some thought that the snakes of St. Patrick had swallowed the two sisters for having violated the site by climbing it on the feast day of Holy Thursday (Ascension Day). Many held the view however, that like the Ascension where Jesus, the son of God, had been lifted into heaven, so too had the angels raised up the two sisters to their rightful place!

None knew what had happened on that day to the two sisters, none ever would. All anyone ever knew for fact was that Nellie and Nora Fanning had both started to climb the mountain and had not come down; nor was any trace of their person ever found by the search party.

The unknown truth remained that two sisters aged 99 years climbed up the mountain that Holy Thursday and only two rattlesnakes descended in their place!

~~~

While it's often remarked that places never change to the eyes of those born there, if such places do exist, Portlaw is certainly not one of them! No one born in Portlaw, who immigrated to England before the 'First World War' years and returning in the year 2016, would recognise the place!

The Village Square remained to mark the centre of the town, but the Tannery had long ago closed down and though there was little employment, much house building had taken place to cope with an ever increasing population; making it look a much different place, less quaint and more mundane!

~~~

The day after the death of the two sisters, over four hundred Portlaw residents died of old age, all being centenarians. For the next two weeks, the village had over forty funerals daily. The Department of Health had to employ a Doctor's Surgery with three doctors to cope with the increased demand as the usual pattern of illness and death returned to the village.

Having had no use for an undertaker or coffin maker for almost sixty years, the village joiner took on three apprentices and they worked overtime for the rest of the year, along with the two new undertakers from County Kerry who had been persuaded to offer their professional services.

~~~

After the mysterious disappearance of the two sisters, on the Holy Mountain, the villagers of Portlaw bestowed upon Nellie and Nora Fanning a reverence, more usually reserved for those having lived saintly lives like Mother Teresa.

Portlaw Village became one of the most famous and talked about places in the whole of Ireland and attendance at Sunday Mass tripled, as all the lapsed Catholics took up their faith once more and the few number of Protestants remaining in the village converted to Roman Catholicism.

The parish priest could no longer cope alone with his enlarged church duties and massively increased congregation and so the Bishop of Waterford appointed a second parish priest. His name was Father Joseph Flaherty, whose grandfather, Monsignor Flaherty, had once been parish priest of Portlaw, as well as having been the blood father of Mary Fanning's partner, Doris.

Indeed, the Village of Portlaw became so pious that confessions were now heard on four evenings per week instead of the previous frequency of once fortnightly.

To cut down on the rapid growth in alcohol consumption, the Town Council banned all public houses from opening their doors on any Sunday of the year! Some of the village heavy boozers could not stomach the sudden restriction in licencing hours that they moved to live outside the town completely!

Following their mysterious disappearance, it became widely accepted by the Portlaw community that the two sisters had been born blessed and had died blessed. Talk soon spread of getting them widely recognised by the Vatican and a campaign grew up supporting the beatification and sainthood of Nora Fanning and Nellie Fanning.

During the years ahead, the Catholic Church was to examine numerous alleged miracles, performed by the sisters during their lifetime. Many gave testament to actually having seen the two sisters perform miraculous healings and restoring life to the dying by the laying on of hands. Many other villagers attested to the miracles that their parents and other family members had told them about before they had been born.

A civic order by the Parish Council was made stating that the home of the two sisters be preserved for future generations to visit. Towards this end, the 'Portlaw Town Council' bought the house on 14, William Street. In addition, Portlaw residents paid to have a second grotto erected close to the Village Square, near to the entrance of the old tannery works.

'The Grotto of the Two Sisters' now stood alongside 'The Grotto of The Blessed Virgin', a shrine which had graced the village for many years, and which no Portlaw Catholic ever walked past without blessing themselves with the sign of the cross or kneeling and saying a prayer!

Often today, the Catholic villagers would pray at both grottos. At 'The Grotto of The Blessed Virgin', a statue of the Blessed Virgin stood at its centre, four feet high. At 'The Grotto of The Two Sisters', there stood two statues, each three-foot high, one statue to represent each of the two sisters.

~~~

In the winter of 2016, Ireland, England and the whole of Europe experienced a greater rainfall than had ever visited them previously. Nowhere in the whole of Europe did it rain so hard and so much as in the Village of Portlaw. For forty days and forty nights, the heavens poured down rain nonstop.

Though the rain that poured was concentrated within an area of one square mile, the storm that carried it could be heard sixty miles away. It was even rumoured by the people of County Mayo, that the underground seepage of flood water from Portlaw had created disturbance on the holy mount of Crough Patrick, waking the nest of snakes that Saint Patrick is said to have cast into a deep sleep way back in the fifth century before burying them beneath the mountain base

The forty-day storm was so ferocious that it kept all residents inside their houses for most of the entire period, venturing out only in dire emergency. When the storm weather eventually abated and the villagers emerged from their homes and resumed their daily functions and traditions, the village witnessed something that they would only describe as 'miraculous'.

They visited the grottos above the Village Square to pray and give thanks for their continued safety and for having emerged through the bitter storm just experienced. There they found 'The Grotto of The Blessed Virgin,' exactly as they had last seen it, but as to 'The Grotto of The Two Sisters', that was different from before.

In the spot where previously a statue of each sister had stood, now stood a newly sculpted statue! The two new statues were now twin-headed and the faces of all four heads were of identical likeness.

The twin sisters to Nellie and Nora, who had left them at birth, had miraculously re-joined them in death.

The End.

Copyright William Forde: May, 2016.

Author's Background

William Forde was born in Ireland and currently lives in Haworth, West Yorkshire, England with his wife Sheila Forde. He is the father of five children and is the author of sixty six published books and two musical plays; all of which are now available as E-book publications as well as paperbacks.

One of West Yorkshire's most popular children's authors, his books were publicly read in over 2,000 Yorkshire school assemblies by over 800 famous names and celebrities from the realms of Royalty, Film, Stage, Screen, Politics, Church, Sport, etc between 1990 and 2002. The late Princess Diana used to read his earlier books to her then young children, William and Harry and the late Nelson Mandela once telephoned him to praise an African storybook he had written. Others who have supported his works have included three Princesses, three Prime Ministers, two Presidents and numerous Bishops of the realm. Former Chief Inspector of Schools for Ofsted, Chris Woodhead described his writings to the press as 'high quality literature.'

Forever at the forefront of change, at the age of 18 years, William became the youngest Youth Leader and Trade Union Shop Steward in Great Britain. In 1971, he founded Anger Management in Great Britain and freely gave his courses to the world. Within the next two years, Anger Management courses had mushroomed across the English-speaking world.

During the mid-70s, he introduced Relaxation Training into H.M. Prisons and between 1970 and 1995, he worked in West Yorkshire as a Probation Officer specialising in Relaxation Training, Anger Management, Stress Management and Assertive Training Group Work.

During his years as a Probation Officer in West Yorkshire, he also operated Anger Management techniques, Stress Reduction Programmes and Relaxation Training groups within, Educational establishments, Churches, Community Halls, Probation Offices, Hostels, Hospitals, Psychiatric Units and Old Folk's Homes.

He retired early on the grounds of ill health in 1995 and has since developed his writing career, which witnessed him working with the Minister of Youth and Culture in Jamaica to establish a trans-Atlantic pen-pal project between thirty primary schools in Falmouth, Jamaica and thirty primary schools in Yorkshire.

William was awarded the MBE in the New Year's Honours List of 1995 for his services to West Yorkshire. He has never sought to materially profit from the publication of his books and has allowed all profit from their sales (approx £200,000 between 1990 and 2002) to be given to charity. All profits from his future works will be given in entirety to charitable causes.

Since 2011, he has written 11 romantic novels for adults, which have been published under the generic title of 'Tales from Portlaw', plus 2 strictly for adults novels. 'Rebecca's Revenge' represents his first strictly for adult novel and draws upon his many years of experience in the fields of textile and psychology. 'Come Back Peter' is his second strictly for adults novel, and draws on his many years of experience as a probation officer in West Yorkshire, divorcee and access father.

In 2013, William Forde learned that he had a terminal illness (CLL) for which he is presently undergoing treatment.

More information about the author can be found at his website: www.fordefables.co.uk

Other Books by this Author

Please visit your favourite eBook retailer to discover other books by William Forde:

For the general audience:

'Everyone and Everything'

'Douglas the Dragon': Book 1, 'Douglas the Unloved Dragon'

'Douglas the Dragon': Book 2, 'Douglas gets Angry Again'

'Douglas the Dragon': Book 3, 'Douglas gets the Sneezes'

Douglas the Dragon': Book 4, 'Douglas and Desmorelda'

'Douglas the Dragon Omnibus'(All four Douglas the Dragon stories)

'Douglas the Dragon: Musical Play'

'Sleezy the Fox': Book 1. Sleezy Gets a Second Chance

'Sleezy the Fox': Book 2. Sleezy Becomes an Amazing Scapegoat

'Sleezy the Fox': Book 3. Snoozy Catches Forty Winks

'Sleezy the Fox': Book 4. Gilbert Is Reformed

'Sleezy the Fox Omnibus' (All four Sleezy the Fox stories)

'Annie's Christmas Surprise'

'Annie's Snowman'

'Annie's Pancake'

'Annie's Easter Bunny'

'Annie's Rainbow'

'Annie's Birthday Surprise'

'Annie's Music Box'

'Annie's Seaside Surprise'
'Annie and the Bullfrog'
'Annie and the Magician'
'Annie's Kite'
'Annie's Bonfire'
'Action Annie' (An omnibus of all twelve Annie Books)
'Our World' (A collaborative book of environmental stories by William Forde and Kirklees Primary School children)
'Midnight Fighter'
'Maw'
'Butterworth's Brigade'
'Nancy's Song'
'Tales of Bernard'
'Fighter' (A combined book of 'Midnight Fighter' and 'Maw')
'Tales from the Allotments'
'Robin and the Rubicelle Fusiliers'
'Loss' (A combined book of 'Nancy's Song' and 'Lost Kingdom')
'Lost Lucy'
'Lost Kingdom'
'Lost' (A combined book of 'Lost Lucy 'and 'Lost Kingdom')
'The Valley of The Two Tall Oaks'
'Indian Dreams Come True'
'Two Worlds - One Heart' (A combined book of 'The Valley of The Two Tall Oaks' and 'Indian Dreams Come True')
'Bucket Bill'
'One Love, One Heart' (A combined book of 'The Valley of The Two Tall Oaks' and 'Bucket Bill')
'The Bear with a Sore Head'
'Elephants Cry Too'

'Solo and Solomon'

'Bes'

'Bes' (A combined book of 'The Bear with a Sore Head': 'Elephants Cry Too':' Solo and Solomon': 'Bes')

'Four Crude Dudes and The Land of Hope'

'Two Crude Dames and Horace Catchpole'

'Greed' (A combined book of 'Four Crude Dudes and The Land of Hope' and 'Two Crude Dames and Horace Catchpole')

'The Kilkenny Cat' (a presentational publication for schoolchildren in Falmouth, Jamaica. Written originally as a single book but later revised and incorporated into 'The Kilkenny Cat' Trilogy)

'The Kilkenny Cat: Book One: Truth'

'The Kilkenny Cat: Book Two: Justice'

'The Kilkenny Cat: Book Three: Freedom'

'Sleezy the Fox Play'

Romantic Drama

'Tales from Portlaw Volume One'

'Tales from Portlaw Volume Two – The Priest's Calling Card'

'Tales from Portlaw Volume Three – Bigger and Better'

'Tales from Portlaw Volume Four – The Oldest Woman in the World'

'Tales from Portlaw Volume Five – Sean and Sarah'

'Tales from Portlaw Volume Six – The Alternative Christmas Party'

'Tales from Portlaw Volume Seven – The Life of Liam Lafferty'

'Tales from Portlaw Volume Eight – The Life and Times of Joe Walsh'

'Tales from Portlaw Volume Nine - The Last Dance'

'Tales from Portlaw Volume Ten - The Woman Who Hated Christmas'
'Tales from Portlaw Volume Eleven – Two Sisters'
'Rebecca's Revenge'
'Come Back Peter'

Connect with William Forde

I really appreciate you reading my book! Here are my social media coordinates:

Friend me on FaceBook:
http://faceBook.com/fordefables

Follow me on Twitter:
http://twitter.com/fordefables

Connect on LinkedIn:
uk.linkedin.com/pub/william-forde

Find me at Smashwords author page:
https://www.smashwords.com/profile/view/fordefables

Find me at Amazon author page:
http://www.amazon.co.uk/-/e/B0034NHETU

Find me at Lulu author page:
https://www.lulu.com/shop/search.ep?keyWords=william+forde++&type=

Subscribe to my blog:
http://www.fordefables.co.uk/bills-blog.html

Visit my website: http://www.fordefables.co.uk

.

55920853R00092

Made in the USA
Charleston, SC
08 May 2016